Who's Kissing Him Now . . . ?

Nikki Masters stared at the triple-scoop hot fudge sundae melting in front of her. Robin Fisher leaned across the table and said, "Come on, Nikki. You have to keep your strength up."

Doubt showed in Nikki's blue eyes. "A sundae is going to keep my strength up?" she asked.

"Robin says ice cream can cure anything," Lacey Dupree put in.

The three girls were best friends, and they'd gathered for one purpose: to cheer Nikki up. But she'd barely touched her pizza, and now her ice cream was melting fast. Her boyfriend, Niles Butler, was picking up his old girlfriend at the airport that day.

"Look, guys," Nikki said, "it's not that I don't appreciate what you're doing. But even massive doses of ice cream aren't going to help me today. All I can think about is Niles kissing Gillian right this very minute. . . ."

Books in the RIVER HEIGHTS ™ Series

Available from ARCHWAY Paperbacks

BROKEN HEARTS

C A R O L Y N   K E E N E

AN ARCHWAY PAPERBACK
Published by POCKET BOOKS

New York   London   Toronto   Sydney   Tokyo   Singapore

This book is a work of fiction. Names, characters, places and incidents are either the product of the author's imagination or are used fictitiously. Any resemblance to actual events or locales or persons, living or dead, is entirely coincidental.

AN ARCHWAY PAPERBACK *Original*

An Archway Paperback published by
POCKET BOOKS, a division of Simon & Schuster
1230 Avenue of the Americas, New York, NY 10020

Copyright © 1991 by Simon & Schuster
Produced by Mega-Books of New York, Inc.

ISBN: 0-671-73115-7

First Archway Paperback printing May 1991

10 9 8 7 6 5 4 3 2 1

AN ARCHWAY PAPERBACK and colophon are
registered trademarks of Simon & Schuster.

RIVER HEIGHTS is a trademark of Simon & Schuster.

Cover art by Carla Sormanti

Printed in the U.S.A.

IL 6+

BROKEN HEARTS

 1

Nikki Masters stared at the triple-scoop hot fudge sundae melting in front of her. "I can't," she said.

Robin Fisher leaned across the table at the Loft, the fast-food joint known for its delicious ice-cream concoctions. "Come on, Nikki. You have to keep your strength up."

Doubt showed in Nikki's blue eyes. "A sundae is going to keep my strength up?" she asked.

"That's Robin for you," Lacey Dupree said. "She says ice cream can cure anything."

A mischievous gleam lit Robin's big dark eyes. "Hey, I'd never say anything that stupid. *Hot fudge* cures everything," she declared. "Ice cream only takes care of everything else."

Lacey laughed, but Nikki managed only a small smile. The three girls were best friends, and they'd gathered at the Loft on Saturday afternoon for one purpose—to cheer Nikki up. They'd given her the choice of a movie, shopping, or junk food, and Nikki had picked pizza and hot fudge sundaes. But she'd barely touched her slice at the Pizza Palace, and now her ice cream was melting fast. How could she possibly eat? Her boyfriend, Niles Butler, was picking up his old girlfriend from England at the airport that day.

Robin pointed at one of the scoops of ice cream in Nikki's dish. "Look, I got pistachio for you. It's healthy—nuts are good for you."

"Speaking of nuts," Lacey said, pointedly staring at Robin. Robin responded by shoving her spoon into Lacey's strawberry sundae.

Nikki tried to smile. "Look, guys," she said, "it's not that I don't appreciate what you're doing. But even massive doses of ice cream won't help me today. All I can think about is Niles kissing Gillian hello right this very minute. Picturing it is driving me absolutely crazy!"

Niles Butler, a transfer student from England, was Nikki's new boyfriend. She'd managed to push aside thoughts of his girlfriend back in England, but she couldn't ignore Gillian's existence any longer. The girl was arriving at the Chicago airport at three o'clock that very day!

"Try not to think about it," Lacey said soothingly, her pale blue eyes expressing her worry.

"They're probably just shaking hands," Robin said in an unconvincing tone of voice. She smiled feebly at Nikki and cleaned up the last of her ice cream.

Nikki sat up straighter and played with the end of her blond ponytail nervously. "Did I tell you that Niles's parents and Gillian's are best friends?" she asked.

Lacey and Robin nodded sympathetically.

"The Butlers are all going to pick up Gillian and her parents," Nikki went on. She wound the end of her ponytail around her finger tighter and tighter as she spoke. "They'll all be one big happy family, I guess. At least Gillian's mom and dad decided to stay at the River Inn instead of with the Butlers. I couldn't stand it if Niles and Gillian were in the same house!"

Robin reached over and put her hand on top of Nikki's as it furiously twirled her hair. "It won't help any if you pull all your hair out," she said.

Nikki then began to trace patterns on the paper tablecloth with her spoon. "I was so close to telling Niles that I loved him at the country club last week. Everything was so romantic, so perfect. And then he told me that Gillian was coming. I almost died."

"But you didn't," Lacey pointed out. "And you won't. You'll meet her, you'll be really nice to her, and then she'll go home. And you'll have Niles all to yourself again."

"Right," Robin agreed, running a hand through her short dark hair. "Anyway, what are you worried about? Gillian's no match for you, Masters. She's probably some frump in a baggy tweed skirt and oxfords." Robin pursed her lips and put on a refined British accent. "Oh, I say, Niles, that's perfectly ripping," she imitated. "Cheerio, and all that rot."

The contrast between Robin's fake upper-crust accent and her wild attire was enough to make Nikki and Lacey burst out laughing. Robin was wearing a purple turtleneck with red suspenders, and she had her solar system earrings on. No matter how dire the situation, Robin could always cheer them up.

"Good try, Rob," Nikki said, grinning. "But somehow I don't think Niles would go for the Queen Elizabeth type."

Robin waved her spoon in the air. "Take it from me, Nikki, I have a feeling about this girl. Gillian's idea of a good time is probably pruning rosebushes. Now that Niles has seen how much fun an American girl like you can be, he'll never go back to some stuffy English girl."

Nikki nodded, but she knew Robin was only trying to make her feel better. She stared dubiously at the ice cream in her silvery dish. All three flavors—pistachio, fudge ripple, and raspberry swirl—had melted into a gooey, unappetizing mess.

Nikki sighed. "Let's try the movies next," she suggested.

That night, Karen Jacobs sat stirring her hot chocolate, waiting for it to cool. She and Ben Newhouse were at Mocha and More for a snack after bowling at Mel's Lanes. When the fifties party had been held there for Winter Carnival, she and Ben had discovered bowling. They were both terrible, but they always had a hilarious time. They ate hot dogs and drank sodas and cheered each other on as they threw gutter ball after gutter ball. They both had yet to break a hundred, but they didn't care.

That was what she loved about Ben—even though he was good at a lot of things, he wasn't embarrassed to be bad. He got just as much of a kick out of his inept bowling as his perfect serve in tennis. He was so much fun to be with!

If only, Karen thought, blowing on her hot chocolate, she wasn't so worried tonight. Ben's old girlfriend, Emily Van Patten, had moved back to River Heights from New York City that very day. Ben had been totally in love with Emily before she moved away, and Karen knew that Ben had gone over to Emily's house that afternoon to welcome her back.

There was nobody at River Heights High that

Karen was more jealous of than the stunning model Emily Van Patten. She had a mane of shining blond hair, long legs, and an absolutely gorgeous face. Next to Emily, Karen felt like a little brown mouse. With her frizzy brown hair and hazel eyes, Karen wasn't much competition for Emily, the glamour queen. Karen knew that she could never have snagged Ben if Emily hadn't moved away.

At least Ben hadn't mentioned Emily once all that night. But suddenly Karen wondered if Ben's not mentioning Emily was a bad sign. Ever since they'd left the bowling alley, he'd been kind of quiet. Karen's heartbeat suddenly speeded up. Maybe something *had* happened with Emily.

She took a spoonful of whipped cream and a sip of the rich chocolate. "Mmmm. This is perfect. It's such a cold night."

"Yeah, this should warm us up," Ben agreed.

Do it, Karen urged herself. Bring up the subject, because Ben never will. "So did you see Emily today?" she asked as casually as she could manage.

The change in Ben was immediate. He quickly picked up his cup and took a nervous gulp. "Ow!" he exclaimed, and slammed the cup down on the saucer and took a long sip of cold water. "Burned my mouth," he said to Karen.

"That's too bad," Karen said soothingly, but something told her Ben might have deserved it. "Are you okay?"

Ben flashed his handsome grin, but it looked a little strained. "I'll survive. What were we talking about?"

"Emily," Karen said pointedly.

"Oh. Right." Ben picked up his hot chocolate again, then grimaced and put it down. "I saw her this afternoon."

"How is she?"

"Fine. Well, she's upset about her parents' divorce, naturally. Her mother can be a little pushy about the acting bit, and she wasn't crazy about Emily's decision to move back here and live with her father. That's tough to deal with."

"Mmmm," Karen murmured. Somehow, she didn't buy it. Emily Van Patten was not only gorgeous, she was the most self-assured person Karen had ever seen. It was hard for Karen to picture her being unable to handle anything.

"Emily's a really sensitive person," Ben went on. "She's worried that the kids at school won't accept her since she's been on television and everything."

"Even though the pilot episode of 'Three Strikes' got such lousy reviews?" Karen asked. She couldn't help it. Although the star of the show, Jason Monroe, was a teen heart-throb, the show had bombed in a major way.

"It's still amazing that she was actually on TV," Ben said defensively. "Jason Monroe only wanted the show rewritten to improve it. Emily wasn't dropped because she was bad or anything."

"I'm sure. Well, I don't think she has anything to worry about," Karen said wryly. "The adoration level at school probably won't dip at all."

Ben looked at her sharply. "Maybe if you got to know her, you wouldn't say things like that. Maybe you'd feel a little sorry for her, too."

"Oh, I'm crushed for her," Karen shot back. Then she stared down at her hot chocolate and sighed. "I'm sorry, Ben," she said meekly. "I really don't know Emily that well, but I do have to admit that I'm a little jealous of her. I'm afraid you'll want to start dating her again. Silly, huh?"

She raised her focus from the tabletop to Ben's face and smiled. His eyes slid away from hers, and he became fascinated with an older couple sitting by the door.

Karen felt her face drain of color. Something was very wrong. "Ben? Isn't that silly of me?"

Ben swallowed. "Actually, I wanted to talk about that. Seeing her this afternoon . . . well, it kind of changed things. The thing is, Karen, I guess I *would* like to date Emily again."

It was like waking up and finding out a

nightmare was actually happening. Pain knifed through Karen, and she desperately fought to hold back her tears. She couldn't lose it in public!

"So you want to break up?" she managed to ask.

"No, Karen," Ben said softly. He leaned forward across the small table, his brown eyes concerned. "I don't want to break up."

"I—I don't understand," Karen stammered. "You want to date Emily."

Ben looked down and played with his napkin. "I was really in love with her, Karen. That's kind of hard to forget. And she needs me now——"

"Are you going for a merit badge or something, Ben?" Karen snapped, interrupting him. "You're a little old to join the Boy Scouts."

Ben winced. "That's not what I mean. Look, I don't blame you for being upset——"

"Thank you," Karen said. "I appreciate that."

"Karen," Ben said desperately, "please, please listen to me. Emily broke up with me, and now I don't know if I'm still in love with her. I don't know how I feel about her."

"Oh, Ben." Karen's eyes filled with tears, and she looked down so Ben wouldn't see them. She couldn't bear hearing Ben say he might be in love with someone else.

"What I *do* know," Ben continued, "is that I care about you. I really do, Karen. These past few weeks have been fantastic."

"If they've been so fantastic, why do you want to see Emily?" Karen asked, swallowing against the painful lump in her throat.

Ben looked miserable. "I care about *both* of you. I'm confused. I mean, I don't know how to handle this. I don't want to hurt either of you. Emily wants to try again. How could I say no?"

"Like this," Karen said flatly, lifting her head to meet his eyes. "No."

Ben stared at his hands. "Listen, I know I have no right to ask this, but I need some time. I have to figure out how I feel. So I was hoping you'd keep on seeing me, even though I'll be dating Emily, too. You can date other guys. That will give us both a chance to see how we feel."

Karen didn't know what to say. She already knew how she felt about Ben — she loved him. Who else would she possibly want to go out with? But if she didn't agree to his proposal, she could lose him for good. It would be torture to know he was dating Emily, but a worse torture would be seeing them together and not dating him herself.

"Please, Karen," Ben said, taking her hand. "I don't want to lose you. Will you try it my way?"

Karen gulped back the tidal wave of tears she could feel welling up behind her eyes. What choice did she have? She loved Ben too much to lose him completely. "All right, Ben," she said. "I'll do it."

2

On Sunday morning Brittany Tate pulled her father's car into the country club parking lot. After she got out and slammed the door, a blast of cold air hit her. Brittany caught her breath before starting across the parking lot. After she took a couple of steps, some grit kicked up by the wind flew into her face.

"Drat," Brittany murmured. Her eyes started to tear, and she hurried toward the country club entrance. The day had barely begun, and she was already in a bad mood. She hadn't wanted to come to the country club for brunch at all, but one of her two best friends, Kim Bishop, had insisted.

Brittany paused to dig in her handbag for a tissue to wipe her streaming eyes. It wasn't

that she didn't like the country club. She
loved it. But ever since her date with Chip
Worthington and his parents there the past
Saturday night, she hadn't been back. She'd
left the table immediately after dinner, disgusted by Chip's efforts to turn her into a
younger version of his mother.

Brittany still couldn't believe she'd worn
that frumpy dress and pearls. She liked her
miniskirts and boots. If Chip couldn't handle
the way she really dressed and acted, he could
go back to his boring ex-girlfriend, Missy Henderson. They were perfect for each other. Right
then Brittany would gladly have handed Chip
back to Missy on a silver platter—sterling, of
course.

Chip was such a snob, Brittany thought as
she pushed open the oak doors into the club.
She couldn't have put up with him for very
long, anyway. The next time she saw him, she
was going to fling those stupid pearls of his into
his ugly face. She'd wanted to give them back
on Saturday, but the opportunity never pre-
sented itself. Then she hadn't even allowed
him to drive her home—she'd called her dad
to come for her. Brittany wiped her left eye,
which was still tearing, and looked around for
Kim and her other best friend, Samantha
Daley.

While she waited, she smoothed her new
haircut into place. After a week of living with
her hair a couple of inches shorter on one side,

she'd gathered her courage and gone back to the Clip Shop to finish the haircut. Even though it had been Chip who suggested the new style, Brittany had to admit it did suit her. Now her hair hung straight and shining to her shoulders, bringing out her dark eyes and dramatic cheekbones.

Just then, Brittany saw Missy Henderson with a group of her preppy friends. They were all wearing tennis sweaters and bored expressions. Missy's small blue eyes narrowed when she saw Brittany. A spark of meanness in them made Brittany's skin break out in goose bumps.

"I guess she still hasn't gotten over being dumped," Missy said, loud enough for Brittany to hear. "Chip dropped her a week ago, and she's still crying her eyes out."

"Poor thing," one of Missy's friends said, not meaning it at all.

Brittany's face flushed angrily. This was too much! They thought her eyes were watering because of Chip. They'd never believe that she had something in her eye.

Missy's other preppy friend spoke up. "So are you and Chip back together, Missy?" she asked.

Brittany sneaked a look at Missy. Now it was the little snob's turn to blush. She lowered her voice, but Brittany had excellent hearing. "Well," Missy drawled, "he begged me to forgive him. He said that that Tate girl had just thrown herself at him and that he never cared for her at all. It only took a few dates for him to realize what a nothing she was."

That was a barefaced lie! Chip had been phoning Brittany all week, but she'd refused to take his calls. He was still crazy about her! Trying not to hurry, Brittany strolled into the first room adjoining the hall. Her cheeks were burning, and she felt so angry she was shaking and barely noticed that her eye had stopped tearing.

Brittany stared with unseeing eyes at a wall covered with plaques. She had never entered this particular room before—it was always full of men too ancient to interest her. It was where the older male members of the club played cards and had boring conversations about stocks and yachts. Out of the corner of her eye, she could see the stir her entry had produced. Eyes peered up at her over lowered newspapers, and at least five throats were cleared.

Brittany didn't care. She decided to wait there until she was sure Missy and her clique had left the front hall. Normally, Brittany wouldn't care what Missy or any of her friends said, but she'd just joined the country club, and it was very important to her. How was she going to be accepted there if Missy was always whispering about what a loser she was?

Brittany stared stonily at the bronze plaques on the wall. Slowly one name began to stand out from all the others. In the lists of original chartered members, tennis and golf championships, and the bequest for the library on the south wing the same name kept turning up. Worthington. Worthington. Worthington.

Worthington! Brittany shook her head. Had she been a little too quick to dump Chip? Especially since the entire country club now thought that *he'd* dumped *her*. She couldn't let Missy get away with the stories she was spreading.

Brittany turned back toward the hall, her embarrassment now forged into steely purpose. If she played her cards right, it would be Missy's turn to be embarrassed. Nobody made a fool out of Brittany Tate. Thank heavens she hadn't given back those pearls. When Brittany next walked into the club, it would be on Chip Worthington's arm.

On Monday morning Nikki pulled her blue Camaro up in front of Robin's house. Robin was outside waiting for her, a bright spot of color against the bare trees and winter lawn. She was wearing orange wool tights and a red minidress underneath an open coat. She ran toward the car as soon as Nikki pulled up.

Robin started talking the second she opened the car door. "Hi, guys. The one day I don't have swim practice before school and I'm probably going to be late for homeroom." She slid into the front seat with a grin for Lacey, who sat in the back. "There's no justice."

Nikki was frowning. "It's my fault, Rob. I took forever to get ready."

"No sweat. We'll make it." Robin checked out Nikki's outfit as they drove toward River Heights High. "Hey, Nikki, the effort was worth it. You look fantastic."

Nikki was wearing a nubby gold sweater over trim corduroy pants of the same color. Soft leather boots rose to midcalf, and her oversize blazer was a deep plum. Her blond hair was freshly washed, and it shone. "Thanks," she said. "You think the colors are okay?"

Lacey's light blue eyes danced. "You're asking someone who wears orange tights with a red dress if you match?"

"Hey," Robin protested, pretending to be hurt. "I can match. I just don't *want* to. Nikki, the colors look great on you. You're going to knock Niles's eyes out."

"I don't think it's Niles's eyes she wants to knock out," Lacey observed.

Robin bounced a little in her seat as she turned to look at Nikki. "Tim Cooper?" she practically squealed. "Well, it's about time. I always knew—"

"Robin!" Nikki stopped her friend. "I don't know where you get your ideas. I keep telling you, Tim and I are ancient history."

"Oh," Robin said meekly. "Of course."

"Nikki is meeting Gillian after school today," Lacey explained.

"Niles called on Sunday to ask me if I'd show her around River Heights," Nikki said, slowing to a stop. "I'm incredibly nervous."

"I can tell," Robin said. "You just stopped at a green light."

"Oh. Sorry." Nikki stepped on the gas as a car honked behind her. "Anyway, I just can't get over how happy Niles sounded. I'm really worried about this now."

"Well, just remember she'll be going back in two weeks," Lacey said. "Niles is staying through the school year now, isn't he?"

"It looks that way," Nikki said. "His father's project for Masters Electronics is incredibly complicated. Anyway, I just don't know how I'm going to act around Gillian. I know she told Niles they should both see other people. But that doesn't mean she'll want to be my best friend. If I were Gillian, I wouldn't be too glad to see me."

"Right," Robin said. "But if you *were* Gillian, you might not want Niles anymore, so if you saw you, you'd think you were a fantastic person and you'd want to be your friend. Right?"

Nikki frowned. "Could you repeat that?"

"Please don't," Lacey said, laughing. "It would still be totally confusing."

Nikki pulled into the River Heights High parking lot. She turned off the ignition and sighed. "It can't be more confusing than this whole situation," she said. "In just a few hours I'm going to try to make my boyfriend's old girlfriend feel comfortable. If that's not a mess, I don't know what is."

Robin frowned at the textbooks in her lap. "Try trigonometry," she said.

"I have tried trig," Nikki said, "and I still know something even worse."

Lacey swung her long red braid over her shoulder. "Uh-oh," she said. "What did you leave out, Masters?"

"There's another reason why Gillian and her parents have come to River Heights," Nikki said gloomily. "Have you ever heard of the Young Players Music Competition?"

"Sure," Robin said. "It's held every year in Chicago, with kids from all over the world competing. It's really prestigious. Whoever wins gets to play in the Chicago summer Mozart festival."

Nikki nodded. "Well, it's coming up. It's really hard even to get into the competition. The auditions were Saturday and Sunday. And since it's open to students from other countries, too——"

Robin slumped down in her seat. "Oh, no," she moaned. "Don't tell me."

"Gillian tried out yesterday," Nikki said. "Remember I told you she was a violinist? Well, she made it. And," Nikki added dolefully, "knowing Gillian, she'll walk away with first prize. Niles said she's incredibly talented. As a matter of fact, if he says it one more time, I'm going to punch him out."

"You're incredibly talented, too," Lacey said loyally. "You're a terrific actress and a great photographer."

"Thanks, Lacey," Nikki said. It wasn't much consolation, but she appreciated the compliment.

Robin spoke up. "Well, I can think of one good thing about the next two weeks."

Nikki opened her car door. "I can't imagine what," she said.

Robin grinned. "At the end of fourteen days, it'll be over," she said.

At lunch that day the cafeteria seemed noisier than usual. Kids were table-hopping, talking and laughing and throwing wadded-up paper bags from one table to another. Karen weaved through the melee, anxiously searching above the bobbing heads for Ben. Karen and Ben usually ate lunch together. Would he be sitting with Emily Van Patten instead? she worried.

"Karen! Over here!" Karen saw Ellen Ming waving at her across the cafeteria. Teresa D'Amato was sitting with Ellen, and they both pointed to a chair at their table. When Karen hesitated, they only pointed more insistently. With a sigh, she headed toward her friends.

"Thanks for saving me a seat, guys," she

said as she came up. "But I really should look for——"

"Have a seat, kiddo," Teresa said grimly.

Karen felt her knees go weak and she sank into the chair. "Where is he?" she asked in a low voice.

"At Emily's table," Ellen said sympathetically. "Way up at the front, near the cafeteria line."

"I forgot that they used to sit there," Karen said numbly. She shot a quick glance toward the table. She saw Emily first, in a soft pink sweater. Then she saw Ben. He was directly across from her. They were laughing. Suddenly it felt as though a knife were being twisted in Karen's stomach.

"Come on. Eat your sandwich," Ellen advised. "You don't have much time."

"I don't feel hungry," Karen said quietly.

"Don't let Emily see you like this," Teresa urged. "Pretend to eat, at least. You've got to act confident and happy. Ben's not going to want to go out with you if you look sad all the time."

Teresa could be blunt, but she was usually right. Karen began mechanically to unwrap her sandwich.

"So," Teresa said, in an obvious attempt to make conversation, "is it true, Ellen? Did Suzanne make it into the music competition in Chicago?"

Ellen's sister was a talented pianist. Ellen's delicate skin flushed with pride. "Yeah, she did. We're all so excited."

"That's incredible," Teresa said. "I'll have to congratulate her when I see her." She threw a meaningful glance at Karen, but Karen was still staring silently across the cafeteria.

Ellen exchanged glances with Teresa. "You'll never guess what else happened with Suzanne," she said. "The vote for that Freshman Council member was this morning. I was so worried about it, since Suzanne had decided to run. I was positive she'd have a breakdown if she lost. Anyway, she rushed up to me in the hall after fourth period, all smiles. I figured she'd won, so I congratulated her. She hadn't won at all. She lost!"

"You're kidding!" Teresa said. "Why was she so happy?"

Ellen giggled. "Because she lost by only four votes. For Suzanne, that was a victory. You know how shy she is. But she ran a good campaign, and lots of kids voted for her. She's not upset at all. I wasted the entire weekend worrying about her. Isn't that funny, Karen? Whoever thought that losing could make someone so happy?"

Karen was busy watching Ben go back in line to fetch a diet soda. Ben didn't drink diet soda, so Karen knew it was for Emily.

"I don't know," Karen said finally. "I don't think losing is all it's cracked up to be."

Ellen's expression changed to one of dismay. "Oh, Karen, I'm so sorry. I didn't mean——"

"I know, Ellen. But I've got to face it. One of us is going to lose Ben, and it looks as if it's probably going to be me."

"With that attitude, it will be," Teresa said. "Come on, Karen. Let that Jacobs brain kick in. Your relationship isn't over yet."

Glumly, Karen took a bite of her sandwich. Teresa was right. She couldn't just give up. She wouldn't sit there day after day and watch Emily steal Ben's heart. She would have to fight back, and to do that she'd need a plan.

3

After the last bell Brittany almost ran to the front entrance of the school. Everything depended on Kim and Samantha not seeing her. If they knew she was taking the bus to Talbot, the exclusive prep school Chip attended, they'd probably tie her up and gag her. Neither of them could stand the guy.

She was hurrying down the front walk when she heard Kim's sharp voice. "Brittany!"

Brittany closed her eyes briefly in frustration. Then she composed her face into a pleasant expression and turned. Kim, Samantha, and Jeremy Pratt, Kim's super-snob boyfriend, were just starting down the front steps. "Hi," Brittany called.

Kim proceeded regally down the walk,

Samantha and Jeremy at her side. Brittany tapped her foot impatiently. Heaven forbid Queen Kim should hurry. Talbot's last period ended a half hour later than River Heights High's, but Brittany had to take the bus all the way out there.

"Where are you rushing off to?" Kim asked, her cool blue eyes sharp with curiosity.

"To Blooms," Brittany lied quickly. "And I'm late." Blooms was her mother's florist shop, and Brittany worked there a couple of afternoons a week.

"We'll stop by later to say hi," Samantha offered. "We're going to the mall."

"Great," Brittany said. "But I have a ton of deliveries this afternoon. You probably won't catch me. Maybe we can talk tonight."

Samantha nodded, her light brown curls bobbing. "Okay."

Brittany was home free. But suddenly Jeremy Pratt's eyes roamed over her curiously. "Whoa. That's some outfit, Brittany. You must be on the prowl again, huh?"

Brittany wanted to strangle Jeremy with his cashmere scarf, but she settled on ignoring him completely. "I've really got to go," she said.

Jeremy's words had done the trick, though. Suspicion flared in Kim's eyes. "Wait a second," Kim said. "Something weird is going on. You never care if you're late for work. And Jeremy's right—what's with the outfit?"

Brittany self-consciously tugged on her black leather skirt. "What do you mean?" she asked. "What's wrong with it?"

"Nothing's *wrong* with it," Samantha jumped in, her cinnamon brown eyes narrowing. "It's fantastic. But isn't it a little, uh, sexy for school and working at Blooms?"

"Really, Brittany," Jeremy said. "It doesn't pay to overdo it. Guys go for the natural look these days."

Brittany gave him a cold look. "Why don't you eat some paste, Jeremy?"

"And isn't that a brand-new gold silk blouse under your jacket?" Kim went on shrewdly. "You usually save something new like that for a date." Her ice blue eyes widened. "Oh, no. Don't tell me Chip 'Old Man' Worthington is back in the picture?"

Samantha's jaw dropped. "Please don't tell us that."

"Really," Jeremy said. "I mean, it's too soon to be *desperate,* Brittany."

Brittany knew it was time to go. "Oh, for heaven's sake," she said airily. "I wear something new and you guys jump to conclusions. Listen, my slave driver of a mother is probably watching the clock. I'm out of here." She waggled her fingers in a goodbye wave.

Hugging her books, Brittany ran to the bus stop, feeling thankful that a bus was just pulling up. She hopped on and found a seat, her heart pounding. That was close! Eventually she'd have to drop the bombshell that she and Chip were back together, of course, but not until she knew for sure.

When she got to Talbot, Brittany positioned herself immediately outside the front door. Blue-blazered boys spilled out the doors, most of them stopping briefly to give her a second look. Brittany ignored them. She'd chosen her outfit with Chip in mind.

Her black leather skirt was typically what Chip would criticize as being too sexy. He'd never let her wear it to the country club or to meet his parents. And there was no way she'd put the pearls he gave her around her neck again. Not that she'd return them, of course. She'd let them gather dust in her jewelry box rather than give them back, she had decided after thinking about them for the past day. Brittany might be willing to take the guy back, but she wasn't a pushover. This time, he'd have to accept her the way she was.

Finally Chip came out of the door. He was frowning against the bright sun as he drew a coat on over his blue Talbot blazer. With his arm halfway in the sleeve, he spotted Brittany. He stopped and stared. Brittany had to admire the way he quickly recovered and finished putting on his coat. His step was unhurried as he came toward her. He probably had taken lessons from Kim.

"Well, well, if it isn't Miss Tate," he said mockingly. "What brings you all the way to Talbot?"

Brittany steadily fixed her dark eyes on him. "Well, well, *Mister* Worthington. Why don't you guess?"

"You came to see me?" Chip asked, pointing to himself. "It can't be. You've ignored my phone calls for a week."

"Why were you calling me?" Brittany asked, shaking her head so that her new haircut would show to good advantage.

"I had some crazy idea that I should apologize," Chip said in his usual offhand tone. He shrugged. "I know why you left me sitting there with my parents last weekend. Maybe I was a little pushy."

"More than a little," Brittany agreed.

"So maybe I have one flaw," Chip said. "I worry too much about what my parents think."

"As long as you have only *one* flaw, Chip," Brittany said, her eyes twinkling.

"Perfection can be boring, Brittany," he returned quickly. "Except in your case, of course," he added, smiling.

It was the opening she wanted. "If I'm so perfect," Brittany pointed out, "maybe you shouldn't try to change me."

"Maybe you're right. Especially when you look as good as you do today."

Brittany smiled and her dark gaze locked on his. "Thank you," she said.

"I take it," Chip murmured, "this means I'm forgiven?"

"You're forgiven," Brittany said softly. "For now."

"Tell me, Brittany," Chip said suddenly. "Why didn't you take just one of my calls, or call me back? You could have saved yourself a long bus ride."

A slow smile spread over Brittany's face. She took a step closer to Chip. "Because," she murmured, "if I called you, I couldn't do this."

Brittany gently grabbed the lapels of Chip's coat. A delighted smile spread across his face as she drew him closer and closer to her. Then she softly placed her lips against his.

"I see what you mean," Chip said as she drew back. "It's too bad Alexander Graham Bell ever invented the thing at all."

Nikki's steps dragged as she walked down the hallway at school. Gillian was taking the bus to school to meet her and Niles, and then they would all pile into Nikki's car. It was dumb, but Nikki felt like postponing the inevitable a little bit longer.

Suddenly a voice interrupted her thoughts. "Nikki?"

Nikki stopped. She didn't have to turn around to know who had called to her. She would have recognized Tim Cooper's voice anywhere. Tim was wearing a black turtleneck sweater that turned his gray eyes silvery. His brown hair was tousled, giving him a slightly rumpled look. Then he flashed the grin that used to make her go weak in the knees. Funny how it still could. Just reflex, she guessed.

"I wanted to talk to you about the talent contest," Tim said. "Do you have a minute?"

"Sure," Nikki said. She wasn't anxious to get outside, that was for sure.

Tim leaned against the wall. "I was wondering if you'd like to do a scene with me for the contest. I haven't been on stage in a while, and I miss it," he confessed with a grin.

Tim and Nikki had played the young lovers in the River Heights High production of *Our Town*. Tim had been George Gibbs, and Nikki, Emily Webb. That had been when they were still dating. As a matter of fact, the pressures of the play had been one of the main reasons they broke up.

Nikki hesitated. She knew that Tim had been seeing Lara Bennett lately. The sophomore was in drama club, too, and she'd had a crush on Tim since the *Our Town* production. Seeing the two of them together still gave Nikki a pang sometimes. "What about Lara?" she asked.

"I'm asking *you,*" Tim said steadily, his eyes never leaving her face. Nikki had forgotten how intense Tim could be. Niles was so light and charming. Had she ever seen a serious side to him? she wondered. With Tim, she'd always known what his passions were. His acting—and her.

"Nikki?" Tim prompted.

Nikki felt herself blushing. She'd been standing there, staring at Tim. To cover her confusion, she asked briskly, "What did you have in mind?"

"I think you'd be perfect for the part of Rita in *The Blue Moon Luncheonette*. Do you know the play?"

Nikki nodded. The two-character play had been a smash hit off-Broadway in New York a few years earlier. It had moved to Broadway and then won a Tony award.

"There's this great scene in it," Tim went on. He pushed off the wall as his enthusiasm grew. "I think it could be wonderful. It's short, but very dramatic. I really think it would be perfect for us."

"Well . . ." Nikki stalled. She didn't know if working with Tim was such a good idea. She quickly glanced at her watch. "Listen, Tim, I really have to go. Can we talk again another time?"

"Sure. But let me give you this." Tim slid a slender book out of his knapsack and handed it to her. "Here's a copy of the play. I've marked the pages I'm talking about. Why don't you read the play and let me know? We should begin rehearsing as soon as possible."

"Okay." Nikki stuffed the book in her tote

bag. "Well, 'bye. I'll try to talk to you by tomorrow."

"Right," Tim said.

He didn't move. Nikki nodded nervously, then headed down the hall. When she sneaked a look behind her, Tim was still standing in the same position, watching her.

She turned the corner with relief and almost ran toward the school exit. She had other things to worry about, she scolded herself. Why was she wasting time being nervous about Tim?

As she started down the front steps, her eyes were drawn to a striking-looking girl standing beside an oak tree. The girl was standing with Niles. Nikki's steps faltered. This had to be Gillian!

Some frumpy classical violinist, Nikki thought with a sinking heart. Gillian looked like a rock star. Her red hair was cut in a thirties retro style, chin-length and side-parted. She was wearing a black leather jacket, a black miniskirt, tights, and flat-heeled black suede boots that covered her knees. She looked devastatingly chic and much too sexy.

As Nikki approached, Niles saw her and broke into a huge grin. "Nikki! At last. This is Gillian St. James. Gillian, this is my good friend Nikki Masters."

Gillian immediately stuck out her hand. "I'm so very pleased to meet you, Nikki," she said in a crisp British accent. "Niles has told me so much about you." Her green eyes were widely spaced and flecked with gold, and they beamed with honest friendliness. Nikki saw an adorable sprinkling of light freckles on Gillian's delicate nose.

"I'm glad to meet you, too," Nikki said, shaking Gillian's hand. She didn't usually shake hands with people her own age, but she guessed that English people did. It was a nice custom, Nikki decided. It gave her a few seconds to study Gillian without seeming to be rude. Now she understood why people always raved about English girls' complexions. How had all that dreary fog and mist made Gillian's skin so creamy?

"This is fantastic," Niles said, his eyes darting from one girl to the other.

Nikki smiled nervously, and Gillian gave her a genuine grin. "I'm quite excited," she said, linking her arm with Nikki's impulsively. "I can't wait to see my first American mall. That is where we are going, isn't it? Niles said we could."

"Well, let's get started," Nikki said. As she led the way to her car, she felt more confused than ever. She might actually *like* Gillian. She seemed to be a really sincere, fun person. If her sophisticated looks were a little intimidating, they were softened by one of the most infectious grins Nikki had ever seen.

Nikki felt like groaning as she unlocked the door of her Camaro for Gillian. What was she going to do now? It would have been so much easier if she had disliked Gillian, or if Gillian had been distant or cold. Finding out that Gillian was a nice person only made Nikki more miserable.

Ellen had urged Karen to come with her to the Pizza Palace after school. Ellen was going with Kevin Hoffman, whom she had started dating again — and very seriously. But Karen refused the offer. She knew Ellen was trying to cheer her up, but what if Karen saw Emily and Ben there?

That thought made Karen want to curl up and die. She had a lot of work to do for the school paper, the *Record,* but she couldn't face it. All she wanted to do was go home and crawl into bed.

Luckily no one was home when she got there. She went straight to her room. At first she tried to concentrate on her homework, but she kept seeing Emily's long blond hair and perfect smile. She turned on the TV, but that only made her think of Emily and her sitcom. Finally Karen was reduced to doing chores.

As she washed spinach for a salad and set the table for dinner, Karen mentally kicked herself. She shouldn't be mooning around the house like a lovesick idiot. She had promised herself at lunch that she wouldn't roll over and play dead while Emily Van Patten stole Ben away from her. She had to come up with a plan!

First of all, Karen decided as she took out the broom and began to sweep the kitchen floor, she knew she'd have to fight for him. But how?

Karen frowned and paused to lean on the broom. Emily was very intimidating, it was true. She had star quality. Next to the willowy blond beauty, Karen felt like a sturdy, boring oak. She couldn't very well grow long gorgeous hair and get an acting job on a television sitcom or appear in zillions of magazine ads. She had to concentrate on what she did have, what she had that Emily didn't. Better grades was her only answer.

Wait a second. Karen straightened up suddenly. Maybe she had something there. Whenever she had to write a term paper or study for a test, she worked incredibly hard. She did research, stayed up late, got up early, and concentrated on her material. Why couldn't she approach this problem the same way?

Emily didn't have to work at being perfect. It came naturally to her. Karen would just have to try harder. She'd work as hard as she'd ever worked in her life. She'd turn herself into the Perfect Girlfriend.

Ben would see that he couldn't do without her. Even without Emily's flash and style, Karen could still win. She smiled for the first time in days as her brain buzzed with strategies. Emily Van Patten might just face some tough competition.

 **4**

Everything about the mall delighted Gillian. They had stopped in lots of shops, and Gillian had purchased a T-shirt and a bright orange baseball cap, which she was wearing. She'd already sampled a burrito, a bagel, and frozen yogurt. Now she was standing transfixed in front of a soft pretzel wagon.

"I'd love to eat one, but I'd better not," Gillian said with a rueful grin. "Niles has told me so much about American pizza that I don't want to spoil my appetite."

"You could probably eat three of those pretzels and still be able to split a pie with us," Niles teased. "And then you'd wash it down with a milk shake and say, 'How about some tandoori chicken?'"

Gillian burst out laughing. "You're just awful," she said affectionately to Niles. She turned to Nikki. "Niles and I used to eat tons of Indian food," she said. "I could eat it for breakfast, lunch, and dinner. Remember that time I ordered three helpings of chana bajee, Niles? You almost choked on your chutney."

Niles laughed. "And then you finished off the rest of the nan, along with my curry," he said.

"Have you ever had Indian food, Nikki?" Gillian asked.

"No, I haven't," Nikki said in a small voice. She felt so left out! She had never heard of the foods Gillian was talking about. River Heights wasn't exactly the cuisine capital of the world.

All afternoon Niles and Gillian had talked about London and the things they used to do there. They tried to include Nikki, of course. Either Niles or Gillian would explain what they were talking about or tell her that she simply *had* to come to London to see Hyde Park or Harrod's, the big department store, or walk along the Thames River.

Gillian turned to Nikki. "When you come to visit, I'm going to take you straight into London to my favorite place. In England, we eat Indian food as you eat pizza or Chinese food. It's cheap and delicious. You'll love it!"

"Speaking of pizza," Niles said, linking arms with Nikki on one side and Gillian on the other, "don't you think it's about time to eat some?"

"I thought you'd never ask," Gillian said with a laugh. "Lead on, you two."

Nikki felt a little cheered at the suggestion. At least at the Pizza Palace she'd get some moral support. Robin and Calvin had promised to meet them there. Lacey would join them for a little while before she had to go to work at Platters. Her two friends were almost as eager to meet Gillian as Nikki had been. Maybe with all her friends around her, Nikki would stop feeling as if *she* were from a foreign country.

When they pushed open the door to the Pizza Palace, they were met by a noisy, boisterous crowd. It seemed as though everyone had decided to come that afternoon. Ellen Ming and Teresa D'Amato were squeezed into a tiny table with Kevin Hoffman and Martin Ives. Brittany Tate was with Chip Worthington, who didn't look very happy to be in a River Heights High hangout.

Nikki noticed right away that conversation stopped and almost everyone looked up when she entered with Niles and Gillian. Niles's old girlfriend could certainly turn heads. The next day everyone at River Heights High would be buzzing about Nikki Masters's competition.

Nikki was silent as her friends chatted and laughed over their pizza. She barely said hello when anyone, which included practically everyone there, came over to be introduced to Gillian. Even Robin seemed to like the English girl. She talked about clothes with Gillian as though they were old friends.

Gillian ate two slices of pizza, one of them heaped with sausage and peppers. Finally, she pushed away her empty plate. "Oof," she said, patting her flat stomach. "I couldn't eat another bite."

"Tell us about the music competition you're going to be in, Gillian," Calvin said, reaching for another slice.

"Oh, I never thought I'd get in," Gillian said. "Niles was the one who talked me into auditioning. I was absolutely shocked when I was accepted."

"You'll be fantastic," Niles said. "And I'll be in the audience cheering you on."

At least that was one thing she'd be spared, Nikki thought, taking a sip of soda. She wouldn't have to witness Gillian's moment of glory on the stage at Orchestra Hall in Chicago. There was no way she wanted to see that!

Gillian leaned forward. "But I want to know all about River Heights High. Niles has told me of all the fun you have. Your Winter Carnival sounded fantastic. What's coming up next?"

Robin shot up in her seat. "That reminds me!" she said excitedly. "The talent contest! I've decided I'm going to enter." She turned to Gillian. "The school has an annual talent contest," she explained. "The tryouts aren't as grueling as yours, of course, but they're pretty tough. The contest always has some good acts in it, and maybe this year I'll be one of them!"

Calvin and Nikki looked at each other, then at Robin. They both knew Robin very well. Did she possess some hidden talent they weren't aware of?

"Oh, how exciting," Gillian said. "What are you going to do?"

"Yes, what are you going to do, Fisher?" Calvin asked. "Swim laps?"

Robin punched him on the arm. "No, silly. I'm going to sing."

Nikki and Calvin exchanged glances again. "Sing?" Nikki asked, opening her mouth for the first time. "I didn't know you could sing."

"Neither did I," Calvin said. "And I've heard you."

"Of *course* I can sing!" Robin said, clearly hurt. "I just need backup, or I go a little flat. Listen, I'll need your help, Nikki. I want some pointers on stage presence and things like that. I've already started to practice. I'm doing this song, 'You're a Big Fat Zero, but I Really Like Your Face.'"

Gillian gave a peal of laughter. "I love that song!" she exclaimed. "You'll be terrific."

"Thanks," Robin said with a quelling glance at Nikki and Calvin.

Nikki rushed in quickly. "I'm sure you'll be great, Rob."

"Great," Calvin repeated doubtfully.

Just then Lacey arrived. She looked frazzled as she slid into a chair. "Sorry I'm late. And I can't stay long," she said breathlessly. "But I had to go over some notes and stuff with Ms. Rose." Lacey sighed. "Ellen did a great job handling my class secretary duties while I was spending so much time with Rick at the hospital, but I'm really far behind."

Nikki looked at her friend sympathetically. "Don't worry, Lacey," she said. "I'm sure you'll catch up. The important thing is that Rick's so much better."

Lacey nodded, biting her lip, and Niles introduced her to Gillian. Robin leaned over to Nikki. "Gillian's terrific," she whispered.

Nikki frowned. She'd had enough of Niles drooling over Gillian. She didn't need one of her best friends to fawn over her, too! "I know," she whispered back.

Nikki tried to smile as she turned back to the group. Lacey tilted her head in Gillian's direction and raised her eyebrows. Nikki knew what the gesture meant: Wow!

Nikki felt like bursting into tears. What chance did she have to hold on to Niles when even her own best friends were won over by the amazing Gillian?

The next morning Karen got up an hour early. She washed her hair and twisted it into soft curlers. On one Saturday-night date, she'd worn her hair in big soft waves, instead of the tight frizzy curls she naturally possessed. Ben had loved the waves. She scurried downstairs and got out eggs, flour, walnuts, and chocolate. She knew that brownies were Ben's favorites, and she wanted them to be absolutely perfect.

While the brownies were baking, she ironed her prettiest blouse. She would wear the white blouse with her full red wool skirt and add a wide black belt. She'd tried the outfit on the night before, and it had looked great. The skirt was old, but she'd taken the hem up so that it swirled gracefully a few inches above her knees. The addition of the wide belt made her waist look tiny. Until she had a chance to cajole some money out of her mother for new clothes, the outfit would have to do. A diet wouldn't hurt, either. Emily was mannequin slim. Karen resolved to eat just a container of yogurt or cottage cheese for lunch every day.

She heard the buzzer go off for the brownies while she was taking the curlers out in her bedroom. Karen ran downstairs with her hair half done. Her mother was standing at the kitchen table, leafing through the morning paper and drinking her coffee. She raised her head in surprise.

"Why are you cooking so early, Karen?" she asked. "And what are you doing to your hair?"

"I made brownies for Ben," Karen said tersely as she slid a toothpick into the brownies to test them. She put on an oven mitt and pulled out the brownies to cool.

"I guess the hair is for Ben, too," her mother said with a smile.

"Right," Karen answered distractedly. She ran from the kitchen and back up the stairs. Everything depended on getting to school before Emily. She had to see Ben alone!

Quickly Karen pulled out the remaining curlers and brushed her hair. It fell in soft waves to her shoulders. Not bad. She slipped into her black flats and fastened her wide black suede belt. Then she applied a little mascara and some pale rose-colored gloss. She grabbed her books and ran back downstairs. The brownies were cool enough to handle, so she cut them into squares and placed them carefully in a decorative tin lined with wax paper.

Her father usually left for work at the crack of dawn, and her mother would be heading out while Karen was just finishing breakfast. But that day Karen was ready to go when her mother slipped into her coat.

Karen rested the tin and her knapsack on the floor while she slipped into her jacket. "Mom, can I have a ride to school today?"

Mrs. Jacobs glanced at her watch. "Sure, Karen. Do you have an early meeting?"

"Yes," Karen hedged. She didn't want to tell her mother about Ben and Emily. Mrs. Jacobs thought Ben was the best thing since pocket calculators.

Karen clutched her books and stared out the

window during the ride to school. She was so nervous, and the ride was too short. Before Karen knew it, her mother was pulling into the parking lot.

"Thanks, Mom," Karen said. She glanced quickly at the quad, but didn't see Ben.

Her mother frowned. "Karen? Is everything okay, sweetie? You seem a little nervous today."

"Everything's fine, Mom. Thanks again for the ride. I'll see you tonight." Karen slid out of the car and closed the door quickly. She started up the concrete walk. Not many kids were at school yet. Usually she met Ben on the quad, but she knew that sometimes he came early and went to the student council room to do some work. She was counting on that.

With her heart beating swiftly, Karen climbed the stairs to the second floor of the school. She walked down the hall and tentatively pushed open the door to the student council room. Ben was sitting at a table, his back to her. He was hunched over the old typewriter they kept in the office. Karen's heart leapt. She slipped out of her jacket and tossed it on a chair so Ben could see her outfit.

"Hi, Ben."

He turned. When he saw her, a grin immediately flashed across his handsome face. "Karen! You're here early. Hey, you look great."

"Thanks." Karen walked closer and handed him the tin. "I baked you some brownies," she said.

Ben looked surprised as he took the tin. "Brownies? Why did you do that?"

"Because I was thinking about you," Karen said softly.

"Oh. Well, thanks."

"Have one," Karen urged.

"Well, I already had breakfast, but sure," Ben said heartily. He opened the tin and took out a brownie. He took a big bite. Suddenly his face changed.

"What is it?" Karen asked nervously. "Aren't they any good?"

Ben chewed while his expression registered distaste. "They're great," he said. "But they have walnuts in them."

"So?"

"I'm allergic to walnuts," Ben said, carefully extracting a nut from his mouth. "I break out in spots. But it was really nice of you, Karen. I'll just pick the walnuts out. They're really delicious. Honest." He placed the rest of the brownie back in the tin.

"I'm so sorry, Ben," Karen said. She felt like crying.

"Karen, relax. It's no big deal. I love the brownies. I shouldn't have mentioned the walnuts. I'm just a little worried about this term paper," Ben said, frowning. "It's due tomorrow, and you know what a slow typist I am. I'll be up all night tonight.''

Here it was—the perfect opportunity for the Perfect Girlfriend. "Let me type it for you, Ben," Karen breathed. "I'd love to, honest.''

Ben shook his head. "It's fifteen pages long, Karen. I couldn't let you do it. It's my responsibility.''

"But it's just a typing job," Karen said. "I'm a fast typist, you know that. It will take me half the time.''

Ben looked doubtful. "What about your schoolwork?''

"No sweat. I'm completely caught up." She wasn't prepared for her chemistry quiz the next day, but she could study for that after she finished typing the paper. The work she had to do for the *Record* could wait.

Ben's frown grew deeper. "I don't know . . .''

"Well, I do. I'm going to do it. It's ridiculous for you to hunt and peck for hours when I can whiz along." Suddenly Karen had an inspiration. "Why don't you show me your draft at lunch today? We can go over it so that I know exactly what I'll be doing.''

"Okay," Ben said reluctantly. "I wanted to have lunch with you, anyway. But are you sure you want to type this?''

She was going to have lunch with Ben! She

wouldn't have to sit with Ellen and Terry, watching Ben at Emily's table. Emily would be the one to feel hurt and jealous. And after Karen typed Ben's paper, she'd have another point on her side.

"I'm sure," Karen said decisively.

 5

The news came over the PA at the end of
homeroom. Nikki was doodling in her notebook when the principal, Mr. Meacham,
announced that Suzanne Ming had made it into
the prestigious Young Players Music Competition.

"In honor of Suzanne's remarkable achieve-
ment, I've made some special arrangements,"
Mr. Meacham said, his voice sounding tinny
through the loudspeaker. Nikki drew a mustache on the face of the short-haired girl she
was sketching. The sketch bore a remarkable
resemblance to Gillian St. James.

"Suzanne's performance will be next Saturday afternoon," Mr. Meacham went on. Funny, Nikki thought distractedly, Gillian's

49

performance was on Saturday afternoon, too. Thank heavens Nikki wouldn't have to go. Niles was driving to Chicago with Gillian's parents and his own, and there wouldn't be room in the car for Nikki.

"So," Mr. Meacham concluded, "I've arranged for buses to be available Saturday morning for any student who wishes to attend. Mrs. Sexton and Mr. Cale from the music department have agreed to chaperon. Sign-up sheets will be posted outside the music room."

Nikki's pen had stopped drawing somewhere in the middle of Mr. Meacham's announcement. She sat bolt upright, staring at the mesh of the PA box. How could this be happening to her? There was no way she could get out of going to the music competition now!

"Hey, Nikki." Somebody touched her on the arm. Nikki raised her eyes and saw Robin staring down at her. "Everyone has left your homeroom already, Nikki. I was passing by and saw you sitting here. You okay?"

"Oh. Yes—sure. I'm just great." Nikki swept her hair out of her eyes and began to gather up her books. All around her, kids were filing into the room for their first class.

"I wanted to catch you early," Robin said, her dark eyes sparkling as they took off down the hall. "Do you have some time this afternoon? We could go to your house. I want to show you my routine."

"Oh, Robin. I'm sorry, I can't. I'm supposed

to meet Tim. How about tonight?" Tim had asked her to meet him in the greenroom after school. Nikki had read *The Blue Moon Luncheonette* the night before, and she'd told him she'd do the scene with him.

As much as she dreaded the rehearsal with Tim, Nikki was relieved that she wouldn't have to evaluate Robin's performance yet. She had an uneasy feeling that she might have to tell her friend something she wouldn't want to hear—such as she shouldn't enter the contest at all.

Robin hit her head softly with the palm of her hand. "Excuse me, Nikki. I must still have water in my ear from my laps. I thought you said you were meeting Tim Cooper."

With a sigh, Nikki said, "He asked me to be in a scene with him for the talent contest."

Robin thought for a moment. "Well, that makes sense. I mean, you and Tim are the best actors in the junior class. Of course he'd want you to act with him."

"I guess so," Nikki said. "I mean, we've worked together before and everything. Except . . ."

"Except what?"

"Well," Nikki said hesitantly, "I read the play last night. It's really intense. It's about these two people, Rita and Lamont. They used to be lovers, but now they're just friends. They're driving cross-country, and a snowstorm drives them into this deserted luncheonette. They're stuck there for the night, and they're freezing, and to pass the time and get their blood moving they start going over all the things they hated about each other when they were going together. It turns into a huge fight —they nearly kill each other. They do reconcile at the end, though."

"So?" Robin asked. "It sounds pretty cool."

Nikki nodded. "The scene Tim picked for us to do is at the end. It's when they're right in the middle of this passionate argument. Rita even throws a plate of cold canned spaghetti at Lamont. It's all they have to eat. Then they make up. It's so romantic and tender. They even kiss, Rob. And they talk about how even though they drive each other crazy, they're really meant for each other. And though they've tried to have relationships with other people, it just isn't the same. So they might as well accept it—they're in love."

Robin gave a low whistle. "Wow," she said. "I see what you mean. Do you think Tim is trying to tell you something?"

Nikki looked troubled. "No. But part of me can't help wondering. What do you think I should do?"

"Well," Robin said slowly, "I guess you should go ahead and do the scene. Maybe Tim doesn't have an ulterior motive at all."

"Maybe," Nikki said. "But what if he does?"

Robin shook her head. "Nikki, Nikki, Nikki.

What am I going to do with you? I've been telling you for weeks now that your last chapter with Tim hasn't been written. You latched on to Niles a little too fast, in my opinion. I mean, he's a great guy and all, but it was like you just couldn't stand how much you were hurting because of Tim. You were really in love with him. I never believed that you fell out of love that fast."

"You never told me that," Nikki said in surprise. Robin's suggestion made her feel very uneasy.

Robin shrugged. "What was the point? I might have been wrong, and you seemed so happy with Niles. I didn't want to rock the boat. Anyway, what you should be doing now is perfectly obvious."

"It is?" Nikki asked doubtfully.

"You should be thinking very hard," Robin said flatly. "Because this time you'd better be sure how you feel—about Niles *and* Tim."

"But I *am* sure—" Nikki started to say.

Robin interrupted her before she could finish. "Maybe you are," she said softly, "and maybe you're not. This Gillian thing has really freaked you out. Just make sure that you want Niles because *you* want him—not because you're afraid somebody else does."

Nikki didn't know what to say. Robin didn't usually give so much advice. She preferred to joke around a problem. She must really feel strongly about this.

Robin touched her arm lightly. "Hey, Nikki. I didn't mean to get you all churned up. At least doing this scene with Tim might give you a chance to find out how you feel." She looked at the clock in the almost empty hall. "Yikes! I'd better run. I'm really late." Robin grinned and dashed off.

Nikki stared after her friend for a moment. "But what if I'm afraid to find out?" she whispered to herself.

Mr. McNeil paced back and forth energetically while he explained the symbolism in F. Scott Fitzgerald's *The Great Gatsby* to his honors English class. Brittany dutifully scribbled down notes, but she kept one eye on Nikki Masters. The girl was definitely distracted. Her notebook page was as blank as her expression. She had to be brooding about that British bombshell, Gillian St. James.

Brittany could almost feel sorry for her, but then decided it was about time the golden girl had to put up with a little adversity like everybody else. Even Brittany knew she'd feel nervous if Gillian were the ex of a boy she liked.

The normally blasé Chip had been impressed with Gillian, too. Apparently the St. James family was well known in England. Their estate, Parkhurst, was some huge mansion that was on the list of historic places. Chip had told Missy about Gillian, and now the drip was supposedly pining to meet Gillian, too. Missy was an even bigger snob than Chip.

Suddenly Brittany had an inspiration. Maybe what Gillian needed was some good old American hospitality. If Brittany befriended her, she could turn her against Nikki and Missy. Nikki would be humiliated in front of Niles because Brittany would be acting as the friend that Nikki *should* be. And Missy would die knowing Brittany was the one to take Gillian under her wing at the country club.

She knew just how she'd get to be friends with her, too. She had an entrée Missy didn't —her reporter's pad. What would be more natural than to write about Gillian in her column, "Off the Record"? And what better meeting place than the café at the country club? She would call Gillian between classes and set up the appointment.

Brittany bent over her notebook to hide her catlike smile. What a perfect plan. And Mr. McNeil called F. Scott Fitzgerald a genius!

After school Nikki went to the greenroom to meet Tim reluctantly. Everything about the small, shabby room off the stage reminded her of the times she and Tim had met there during the *Our Town* rehearsals. They'd sat and kissed on the dilapidated tweed couch. They'd leafed through the old playbills strewn about on the rickety tables. They'd shared a pizza sitting cross-legged on the faded carpet. Suddenly all

Nikki could remember were the good times — the laughter and kisses, Tim's warm smile. Right then she couldn't remember the jealousy or the anger.

Tim had blocked out the scene for Nikki and him, and they moved through it together. Every move an actor makes on stage is carefully planned in advance. Luckily, the blocking in their scene was a little complicated, so Nikki really had to pay attention. She could forget her confusion and anxiety at actually being in this room alone with Tim.

"Well, I guess we're ready to start reading," Tim said after they'd been through the blocking a few times. "Mrs. Burns said we can use the stage tomorrow after school. If you're free, I mean."

"Sure." Nikki's palms were suddenly damp as she turned back to the beginning of the scene. Tim began to read, and she joined in nervously. Her voice shook a little, but Rita was supposed to be angry, so it added to her reading.

Before she knew it, Nikki was at the part where she had to throw the plate of spaghetti — played by a stained purple and green pillow from the couch — at Tim. After that, he was supposed to sweep her into his arms.

Nikki picked up the pillow and threw it with all her might at Tim. He strode toward her and grasped her by the arms. Nikki felt the warmth of his fingers on her skin like an electric shock.

Her sleeves were pushed up above her elbows, and his fingers slid up her bare forearms. His eyes were like glittering chips of winter ice, and Nikki couldn't look away. She felt mesmerized by Tim's intensity.

Finally he dropped her arms abruptly and stepped back. Now his gray eyes were flat and unreadable. "We can rehearse the kiss another time," he mumbled.

Nikki rubbed her suddenly cold arms. "Right," she said.

Tim cleared his throat. "Maybe we should practice your throwing that spaghetti," he suggested.

"Okay," Nikki said. Relieved, she picked up the pillow. Tim returned to his place on the floor.

"Remember, you're more furious than you've ever been in your life," he said. "You hate me. You think I'm the biggest jerk who ever lived."

Nikki grinned. "That's not too hard."

Instead of grinning back, Tim was serious. "Well, sometimes I can be."

Nikki's smile faded. She hadn't meant what she'd said. Tim might have acted foolishly. He might have pressured her too much about her performance in *Our Town*. He might even have been insensitive to her jealousy of Lara Bennett. But he'd never been a jerk.

"You were never a jerk, Tim," she said softly. "I was only kidding."

Tim stared at her for a long moment. Then he smiled softly. "Let's get back to the scene, Masters. You're angry, remember?"

"Right." Nikki closed her eyes in order to concentrate. She tried to forget about Tim and summon up Rita's fury and disappointment at Lamont. But instead, Nikki flashed back to the cast party at Mrs. Burns's house. She remembered how jealous and angry she'd been when Tim had disappeared with Lara Bennett. She opened her eyes and pitched the pillow as hard as she could at Tim's head.

At that moment the greenroom door behind Tim opened. The pillow sailed through the air with all the force of Nikki's anger and hit Lara Bennett full in the face.

 **6**

Lara's face was bright red as the pillow thumped to the floor. Her hair stuck up on one side where the pillow had hit her. "What's going on?" she asked angrily.

Laughter bubbled up in Nikki, but she desperately tried to squelch it. "I'm sorry, Lara," she said, keeping a straight face with difficulty. "Tim and I were rehearsing a scene. I guess you opened the door at the wrong moment."

"It was an accident," Tim said. Nikki could hear that he was struggling not to laugh, too. She sneaked a peek at him and saw that his gray eyes were twinkling. Nikki felt warm sharing a private joke with him again.

"Well," Lara said, flouncing into the room,

"maybe you should have kept the door open."
Her light green eyes ticked over Nikki, and she
self-consciously smoothed her shiny brown
hair.

She's jealous of *me,* Nikki thought. That was
certainly a turnaround. Only a relatively short
time earlier Nikki had been jealous of Lara.

"Lara, we're not finished yet," Tim said.
The amusement was gone from his voice, and
he sounded annoyed.

"But you said you'd give me a ride home."
Lara pouted. "It's four o'clock."

"Already?" Tim looked at his watch. "I
guess maybe we'd better quit, then. Same time
tomorrow, Nikki?"

Nikki nodded. "Fine." She went over to the
couch to retrieve her tote bag and coat. Lara
and Tim must be getting really close, she
thought. They spent enough time together.

"I'm going to confirm with Mrs. Burns that
we can use the stage tomorrow," Tim said to
Nikki. "Be right back, Lara."

"See you tomorrow, Tim," Nikki called. She
slipped into her coat. Lara perched on the edge
of the couch and picked up Tim's sheepskin-
lined denim jacket. She smoothed it on her lap
as though she were staking out her territory.

"I was rehearsing my act for the talent
contest, too," she told Nikki. "I'm going to
sing 'My Funny Valentine.'"

"That's a great song," Nikki said. She was

glad that Lara was trying to be friendly. She had apparently gotten over Nikki throwing the pillow in her face.

Lara played with the collar of Tim's jacket. "I decided what I wanted to do as soon as Mrs. Burns announced the contest," she said. "Then when Tim got the idea for *The Blue Moon Luncheonette,* I was already committed to my own act."

"Mmm," Nikki murmured. She slipped her tote bag over her shoulder. Lara wasn't being that friendly after all. She was letting Nikki know that she would have been Tim's first choice for Rita. Nikki was only second best. "Well, see you later, Lara," Nikki said.

She walked out of the greenroom and headed quickly down the hall, hoping she wouldn't bump into Tim. He hadn't had any personal motive after all. He'd asked her to do the scene with him only because Lara had already decided to sing.

She should have been relieved to know that she wouldn't need to feel tense and uncertain during the upcoming rehearsals. She could concentrate on Niles again. Nikki pushed open a door leading out of the school and shivered as a blast of cold air hit her face. So why, she wondered as she crossed the parking lot, did Lara's information matter? Why did it make her feel so bad?

* * *

Brittany leaned across the table toward Gillian. "Parkhurst sounds like such a romantic place," she said. "I just adore old houses."

Gillian giggled. "You wouldn't say that in the middle of February. The plumbing creaks and clanks, and you feel as though you'll never be warm again. It's awfully drafty. That's why in the winter we mostly stay in our flat in London."

"Is that where your school is?" Brittany asked.

Gillian nodded. "On weekends, we pile in the car and drive the short distance to Parkhurst, grumbling all the way. We all walk around like mummies in three sweaters and twelve scarves apiece."

Brittany laughed her tinkling laugh, hoping that it carried. Unfortunately, the café at the country club was nearly deserted. Nobody important was there to witness her chumminess with Gillian St. James. Worst of all, Missy Henderson was nowhere in sight.

"Still," Brittany said, returning to the subject, "I'd just love to see your house, even in February."

"Well, you have to come to England someday," Gillian said politely.

Brittany waited for her to ask her to Parkhurst, but Gillian didn't go that far. After all, they'd met only twenty minutes before. "Oh, I'd like to," Brittany said. "I love to travel."

"Some of the old estates have been turned

into hotels, so you can stay overnight in them," Gillian added. Leaning forward slightly, she said in a low tone, "Just be sure to watch out for the ghosts."

"Ghosts!" Brittany exclaimed. "Not really?"

Gillian nodded solemnly. "Parkhurst has one. One of my relatives, actually, from the time of Queen Victoria. His name was William St. James, but we call him Willy. On a dark night, in the middle of winter, if you listen very hard, you can hear him moaning on the north staircase. That's where he died. They say his wife pushed him downstairs."

Brittany laughed uneasily. Was Gillian kidding?

"Well, that's the family story, anyway," Gillian concluded with a sunny smile.

"You've certainly given me some great material for my column," Brittany said.

"I think it's marvelous how you don't need to write anything down," Gillian said admiringly. "You must have an excellent memory."

"It's a journalist's best tool," Brittany said cheerily. Actually, her memory wasn't *that* great, but she'd wanted her meeting with Gillian to appear social, not professional.

Gillian looked at her watch. "This has been delightful, Brittany, but I really should be going. I'm scheduled for a practice at the Westmoor music department." Gillian pronounced the word *"shed*-uled."

She couldn't leave yet! "I love the way you say *scheduled*," Brittany said. "Is that a British pronunciation?" It was a stupid question, but she was desperately trying to keep Gillian sitting for as long as she could.

Gillian was obviously a bit puzzled. "Yes, I suppose it is. I am from Britain, you know," she added dryly.

Just then, over Gillian's red head, Brittany saw Missy and two of her friends enter the room. At last! They headed to the juice bar to order.

Brittany gave another silvery peal of laughter. "It *was* a dumb thing to ask."

Her laugh had the desired effect. Missy glanced over, grimaced when she saw Brittany, and turned back to her friends. Gillian didn't look like Missy's conception of a classy English girl, Brittany knew. That day Gillian was wearing a pair of extravagantly cut black wool trousers. They were pleated at the waist and full in the legs, then tapered tightly at the ankles. With them, Gillian was wearing a white blouse with an oversize Peter Pan collar and a wide black ribbon for a tie. A red chiffon scarf was tied around her head in a floppy bow. Somehow the outfit didn't look ridiculous on her at all.

Brittany stood up. "Well, I won't keep you, Gillian. I know how important your practice is." She reached for her purse and pretended to see Missy for the first time. "Oh, I see some friends of mine," she said. "Let me introduce you."

"Of course," Gillian said politely. She draped her red wool coat, cut like an artist's smock, over her arm.

With a wide smile, Brittany approached Missy and her three friends. "Missy, hi. I want you to meet someone."

Missy's face registered surprise. "Okay," she said flatly. There was no trace of interest in her voice. Brittany saw a shadow briefly cross Gillian's face at Missy's rudeness. Good. Strike one for Missy.

"Missy Henderson, Gillian St. James," Brittany said ringingly. She could have jumped for joy at the expression on Missy's face. The girl looked as if she had just bitten into a lemon.

"I-I'm glad to meet you," Missy stammered.

"So glad to meet *you,*" Gillian said. Her manners were obviously too good for her to be rude to Missy. She stuck out her hand, and Missy stared at it. Finally she took it.

"And this is Trudy Grant and Dee Kingsley," Brittany went on. Chip had introduced her to Missy's friends when they'd bumped into them one day. The two girls swallowed and said hello to Gillian.

Brittany tucked her arm into Gillian's. "Well, we really have to run."

Mission accomplished! Missy's face was practically pea green with envy. With a triumphant smile, Brittany headed for the exit. She waved carelessly over her shoulder as she swept through the double French doors with Gillian. "Cheerio!" she called behind her.

That night in her bedroom Karen took a sip of instant coffee and made a face. She didn't like coffee, but she was starting to get sleepy, and it was barely nine-thirty. She still had ten pages to go on Ben's term paper. Then she had to study for her chemistry quiz the next day.

She would have been farther along with Ben's paper, but she wanted it to be absolutely perfect. If she made even one error, she ripped out the sheet and started all over again. It didn't help that Ben's scrawl was hard to read sometimes, and his grammar wasn't the greatest. Karen did the best she could to correct it and restructure his paragraphs. If Ben got an A thanks to her, he'd have to be grateful!

So far, her plan hadn't been exactly foolproof. At lunch that day in the cafeteria she had had the satisfaction of seeing Emily glance over at them, her pretty face crestfallen. But then, ten minutes later, it seemed as if every male at River Heights High were at Emily's table, and roars of laughter were rolling across the cafeteria toward Karen and Ben. Frowning, Ben had kept checking out Emily's table. So much for capturing his attention.

Karen carefully corrected the verb tense in one of Ben's sentences and continued to type.

Just because Emily had retaliated didn't mean that Karen was going to give up. She'd just try harder.

The telephone rang, and her heart leapt. It was probably Ben, checking up on her progress. Karen reached for the phone and upset the correction fluid she was using to cover up her mistakes. The white liquid spilled all over the page she'd just typed. Quickly she righted the bottle and threw a wad of tissues on top to blot up the excess liquid. Then she picked up the phone.

"Hello?" she said breathlessly.

"Hi, Karen, it's Ellen."

Disappointment thudded through Karen. "Oh, hi. I thought you were at the Loft with Kevin."

"Yes, we went for ice cream," Ellen said. "It was fun. But it's a school night, so I had to come home early. My mom said that you left a message to call."

"Oh, right," Karen said distractedly as she blotted up the correction fluid. "I almost forgot. I've been thinking, Ellen. You always have such great clothes. I really need a dynamite new outfit for my next date with Ben, and I don't want to go to Glad Rags or any of the stores at the mall."

"You mean you want to shop at my mom's store?" Ellen asked doubtfully. Mrs. Ming was the manager of an exclusive boutique downtown, Maison de Mode. "It's awfully expensive. She gets things for me sometimes, but she puts them aside before a big sale. Plus she gets a discount.''

"Well, that's the thing," Karen said hesitantly. "I was wondering if you could get the discount. You know, you could pretend the clothes were for you."

Ellen thought a moment. "I couldn't do that," she said finally. "I mean, I couldn't lie to my mom. But I could ask her if she would buy the outfit for you, the way she does for me. I could go with you."

"Great!" Karen exclaimed. "My mom came through with some money for new clothes, if I promise to do extra chores. I think she expects me to buy a bunch of new things, but I'm going to blow it all on one fantastic outfit. I might as well go for broke, you know?"

"That's exactly what you'll be going for," Ellen said. "Karen, these clothes are really expensive, even with my mom's discount."

"I know, but Ben's worth it. We could go tomorrow after school. If that's okay?"

"Sure," Ellen said. "If you're positive."

"You're a pal," Karen said, looking at her watch. "Listen, Ellen, I'd love to talk, but I don't want to tie up my phone. Ben might be trying to get through."

An awkward pause hummed through the line.

"Ellen?" Karen prodded. "I really should hang up."

"Uh, Karen," Ellen said awkwardly, "I wouldn't worry about Ben trying to reach you right now."

A cold stone dropped to the bottom of Karen's stomach. "What do you mean?"

"He's at the Loft with Emily," Ellen said reluctantly.

"Oh," Karen said in a small voice. She felt as if somebody had just run over her with a Mack truck. "Well, I have to go anyway. I've got tons of work to do."

She said goodbye and hung up quickly, before Ellen could even try to console her. Karen didn't need consolation. Even though she was typing Ben's term paper so he could go out with Emily, she wasn't going to cry or get mad. She was going to get even.

Determinedly, Karen took a swig of cold coffee. She shuddered at the awful taste, but made herself take another gulp. Then she rolled a fresh sheet of paper into her typewriter and got back to work.

7 ~~~

Nikki sat cross-legged on her bed and watched Robin rearrange her furniture. First Robin pushed the flowered armchair to a far corner. Then she carried the desk chair over to the middle of the room. Finally she rolled up one of the scatter rugs to clear a space on the floor.

"Okay," she said to Nikki. "Pretend this is the stage. You sit in the desk chair."

Nikki obediently sat in the desk chair facing the cleared space. "Ready," she said.

Robin fished through her overstuffed purse and came up with a tape. "I got this at the mall," she said. "They have a recording studio there now. They have the backup music, and you sing along. You can choose from hundreds of songs. Then you can buy the tape that you make." Robin put the tape in Nikki's player. "I bought a tape of the backup music without any singing. That way, I'll have the music for the contest."

"Good idea," Nikki said, crossing her fingers in her lap.

"I did my routine for Michael Quinn after school today," Robin said. "He thought I was great."

Not exactly an unbiased opinion, Nikki thought. The sophomore had a super crush on Robin. Michael thought that everything Robin did was amazing. He thought the way she put turquoise shoelaces in her orange high-tops was a work of art.

"Of course, *your* opinion is what really counts," Robin continued. Suddenly she seemed nervous. "This will just give you an idea. I mean, I haven't polished the act or anything. I've just worked out the basic choreography and practiced my singing."

Robin pressed the Play button, and the music blared out. It was a great tune, and Nikki's head nodded to the beat as Robin launched into the opening steps of her routine.

Nikki smiled with relief. Robin could really move! Then she opened her mouth and began to sing.

Nikki kept the smile plastered to her face. Robin had enthusiasm and great delivery. She was nice and loud, but her singing was just plain awful! She roamed all over the scale as though she hoped to hit the right note by accident.

Robin sang her heart out for three choruses. Then she ended with a long, drawn-out note that was very flat. The tape clicked off, and she looked at Nikki expectantly. "Well?" she asked.

Nikki knew she had to choose her words carefully. Robin could be very sensitive. "The choreography is great," she said finally. "I didn't realize what a terrific dancer you were, Robin."

"Thanks," Robin said. "What about—"

"I loved the way you reinforced the funny parts of the song with your body movements," Nikki went on quickly. "It was really inventive. I think you may even be a better dancer than Kim Bishop!"

"Gee, thanks, Nik," Robin said happily. "That's really nice. But what about—"

"And the choice of song was perfect," Nikki interrupted in a cheery tone. "It goes with your personality. And as for stage presence, I don't think you need any tips from me at all."

"But, Nikki," Robin said urgently, "what about my singing?"

This was it—the moment of truth. Nikki swallowed hard. "Your projection is good," she said. "And you have a lot of enthusiasm, Rob." Desperately, Nikki searched for a kind, helpful way to tell Robin that she stank.

Robin suddenly whirled around happily.

"Yahoo!" she exclaimed. "I'm so excited. I can't wait to try out. I've always wanted to be on stage." She ran over to Nikki and hugged her. "You're a pal. Listen, I hate to sing and run, but it's getting late, and I have some homework to do. I've really gotta go."

"Sure," Nikki said dazedly. Robin had jumped to the wrong conclusion. She'd heard only what she wanted to hear. What was Nikki going to do?

With grave misgivings, she watched her friend bound down the stairs. The tryouts were always crowded with students, some of whom weren't even auditioning. They just came to watch. Robin would make a complete fool of herself. How could Nikki find the courage to tell her the awful truth?

When she went to bed that night, Nikki tossed and turned for what seemed like hours. Robin's off-key singing and Gillian's grin kept popping up in her confused dreams. The next morning Nikki woke up way before her alarm went off, glad that the long night was over.

She lay in bed a moment, listening to the hushed morning. The light in her room was different, brighter than usual. Somewhere down the street a car's wheels whined, as though they were spinning. She sleepily made her way to the window and confirmed her guess—it had snowed the night before.

She could see that in the early morning ice had encased every branch on the tree outside her window. The snow was still unmarked by footprints, and it lay like a carpet of diamonds. Nikki's first thought was how beautiful Moon Lake must be. Her fingers itched to hold her camera. She pushed away from the window and hurried to dress.

The sun and early-morning traffic had melted the ice on the road by the time Nikki climbed into her Camaro for the drive to Moon Lake. She had just enough time to shoot one roll before she had to pick up Robin and Lacey for school.

When she got out of the car at the parking lot, she breathed in the crisp air gratefully. She headed down the path toward her favorite spot, her boots making pleasant crunching sounds in the snow. Nikki reached the water's edge and caught her breath. Everything was beautiful and pristine.

She was glad she'd made the effort to come. The hush of a frosty early morning at the lake was just what she needed to drive away the confusion of the week. She concentrated on composing her shots. Maybe if the contrast was good enough, DeeDee would want to print one in the *Record*.

The ice on the lake was snow covered, and it stretched flat and smooth to the horizon.

When she heard footsteps behind her, Nikki turned, startled that someone else should be out so early. She was even more surprised when she saw that it was Niles.

"Hello, sleepyhead," she said, teasing him. "I thought you hated to get up early."

Niles encircled her in a big bear hug and kissed her. His lips felt cold against hers. "You're worth it," he said. "I called to see if you wanted to have breakfast, and your mother told me you'd gone out with your camera. I tried here first. I figured you'd want to shoot the snow on the lake in this light."

"You were right," Nikki said. She was pleased that Niles knew her so well.

"I stopped at a deli and bought some hot chocolate and corn muffins," Niles said. "Will you be ready to have some soon?"

"I'm ready now," Nikki said. "I'm starving, and I'm pretty cold." Even though she was wearing a down-filled jacket, the sun wasn't up enough yet to warm her.

"Come on. The food's in the car." Niles put his arm around her, and they crunched their way back up the path.

The two of them sat in the front seat of Niles's car and peeled the plastic lids off their hot chocolate. "I've been meaning to say something to you, Nikki," Niles said as they took their first sips.

She peered at him over the rim of her cup. Niles looked so serious. "What's that?" Nikki asked, not really wanting to hear his answer. She unwrapped her corn muffin with unsteady fingers, trying to act casual. Did Niles want to break up with her?

"Just thank you," Niles said simply. "Look, I know it can't be easy showing River Heights to my old girlfriend. You've been a brick."

"A brick?" Nikki asked, confused.

Niles laughed. "It's a British expression. It means you've been a really good friend. You've gone beyond the call of duty."

"I didn't do anything," Nikki mumbled.

"Yes, you did. You made Gillian feel welcome. I know it must be a weird situation for you. But Gillian and I are still close. I hope you see why I want us to stay friends."

Nikki nodded. "She is a terrific person, and I like her a lot." She *did* like Gillian, but she knew she'd like her a whole lot better if she wasn't Niles's old girlfriend.

"Did you sign up for the bus trip to Chicago on Saturday?" Niles asked.

To stall, Nikki took a sip of hot chocolate. "Not yet," she said, hedging.

"Well, I hear the buses are filling up fast. You'd better sign up."

"Mmm," Nikki said. She took another long sip of her drink.

Niles grinned at her. "You look so beautiful with that mustache," he teased.

Nikki felt the top of her lip with her tongue. It was covered with chocolate foam. She grinned.

Niles leaned over and gently wiped her mouth with his napkin. Then he kissed her softly. "Don't change that face a bit," he murmured. "I happen to be quite fond of it."

Nikki melted as fast as the marshmallows in her hot chocolate. Niles always said the right thing. She must have been crazy to have thought twice about Tim Cooper again. Of course Niles was the guy for her!

Later that morning Karen was waiting in the quad for Ben to arrive. She could see Emily and a few of her friends standing by the front steps. She was closer to the parking lot, though, so Karen knew she'd see Ben first.

Emily was scanning the parking lot and casting nervous glances at Karen. Karen gave her one long poisonous stare, and Emily tossed her blond hair and returned to her conversation.

Across the lawn, Karen saw Teresa and Ellen get off the school bus together. They were laughing and talking, and their breath steamed in the frosty air.

"Hi, Karen," they both called as they came up.

"What a gorgeous morning," Teresa said.

Karen had been so sleepy she'd barely noticed the weather. She'd stayed up late typing Ben's paper, and then got up early to set her hair and plan her outfit. She should have looked out the window. Underneath her tweed coat, she was wearing only a pink silk shirt and black jeans. She was freezing.

"Are you ready for the quiz today?" Ellen asked her.

"Not really," Karen admitted. She'd barely had time to review the material, but she was pulling pretty good grades in chemistry. Maybe she'd be able to fake her way through the quiz.

"If you want, I can help you in study hall this morning," Ellen offered.

"No, thanks, Ellen," Karen said, peering over Teresa's head at the parking lot. "I noticed last night when I was typing Ben's term paper that his social studies notebook is a mess. He's got all the handout sheets mixed up and stuck in the back. I'm going to put them all in order in a binder for him."

Ellen and Teresa exchanged glances. "You're going to do *what?*" Teresa asked in a high, squeaky voice.

"Look, don't give me a hard time, okay?" Karen said angrily. "I love Ben."

"I know," Teresa said doubtfully. "But do you have to become his slave?"

"Are you sure you're not overdoing things, Karen?" Ellen asked mildly. "I mean, Ben didn't fall for you because of your organizational abilities."

Karen barely heard them. She saw Ben's Toyota pull into the parking lot. She glanced quickly at Emily, who was already starting down the steps. "I've got to go, guys," she said quickly. She dashed off before Teresa or Ellen could say another word.

Ben was locking his Toyota when she caught up to him. "Hi," she said breathlessly. "I brought your term paper. I think it turned out great. An A for sure." She held out the report to him.

Ben grinned. "Hi, Karen. Yes, it *is* a nice morning. I'm doing pretty good, how about you?"

Karen laughed. "I'm sorry. I guess I'm a little excited. It's a great paper, Ben. Here, take a look."

"I'd rather talk to you," Ben said. He took her hand. "I miss you. I didn't expect things to change so much."

Then you were pretty dumb, Karen wanted to say. But Ben was holding her hand, and his brown eyes were so warm. "I know what you mean," she admitted instead. "I miss you, too."

"Do you want to go out Friday night?" Ben asked. "We could try bowling again. I think my game might be improving."

Karen laughed. "That'll be the day. Sure, I'd love to go out Friday." Over Ben's shoulder, she saw Emily lingering by the bike rack, probably waiting to see if Karen would walk away. "Now will you look at your paper?"

Ben dropped her hand and took the term paper. "I hope this didn't take too long."

"Not at all," Karen said cheerfully. Only all night, practically, but he was worth it.

Ben began to read the first page of the paper. Suddenly he stopped and frowned. "This isn't what I wrote," he said.

Karen nodded. "I know. But your opening paragraph was a little confusing. I just fixed it up a bit. It's tighter now."

Ben looked upset as he leafed through the paper. "Karen, I didn't want you to do that. I thought you'd just type what I had. Now I feel like this isn't my work."

"Don't be silly. Of course it's your work," Karen insisted. "I just changed a few teeny things, that's all."

"And this probably took twice as long," Ben went on. "I'm really sorry, Karen. You spent way too much time on this."

"Ben, it's okay," Karen rushed to assure him. "I didn't mind a bit."

"But—" Ben started. Then he stopped and studied the snow at his feet for a moment. "I feel really guilty," he mumbled.

About the paper or dating Emily? Karen wondered, but she wouldn't ask. She had to stay upbeat, fun. "Well, don't," she said. "Because I loved doing it. I'm here for you, Ben."

"Well, next time I'm going to do the typing myself."

Suddenly Karen had an inspiration. "Hey, I've got a great idea," she said eagerly. "Instead of bowling, why don't you come to my house for dinner Friday night? My parents are going out, so we'll have the house to ourselves. I'll cook you a terrific meal."

Ben looked puzzled. "I didn't know you cooked, Karen."

"Sure, all the time." If you counted microwaving a frozen dinner. But a candlelit dinner with Ben could really put her ahead of Emily.

"That sounds great," Ben said. "I'd love to come."

"Fantastic! Come on, let's hit our lockers. It's almost time for the bell." Beaming, Karen swung into step beside Ben. Way over by the front door, she saw a flick of long blond hair as Emily ran inside. The enemy had retreated. But she hadn't surrendered—yet.

8

When Brittany got off the bus, she saw Nikki walking up the path to school with Niles. They were holding hands, so it looked as though Gillian hadn't recaptured Niles. Too bad. Maybe, Brittany thought, she should let Niles know how much she liked his old girlfriend. Niles would appreciate it, Brittany was sure. Of course, Nikki might not, but Brittany couldn't help that.

"Oh, Niles," Brittany said brightly as she approached them. "I met your girlfriend — whoops, I mean your *old* girlfriend — yesterday. She's absolutely fantastic." Brittany felt a gleam of satisfaction when Nikki blanched. She coughed nervously and turned her head away.

"Gillian told me," Niles said. Brittany was glad to see that he had dropped Nikki's hand. "You're writing some sort of article about her?"

"One of my personality profiles," Brittany cooed. "Gillian's an ideal subject. She's so bright and witty. Not to mention gorgeous. You must be very proud of her."

"I am. We're just friends now, though."

"Right," Brittany said. "She told me some wild stories about you two in London!"

Niles became uncomfortable. "We weren't wild," he said.

Nikki's cheeks were stained red with either anger or the cold. "Kim and Samantha are waving at you, Brittany," she said coolly.

Drat those two, Brittany fumed. They *were* waving at her. "Well, 'bye now," she trilled to Niles and Nikki.

Kim and Samantha were waiting with Jeremy Pratt and Kyle Kirkwood at the group's usual meeting place by the steps. "We thought you might want to be rescued from your conversation with Nikki," Kim said.

"Thanks a lot," Brittany said tightly. But she didn't want to make a big deal about it. "Anything new with you guys?" she asked.

"Besides freezing to death, you mean?" Samantha grumbled. She was wearing a down parka, sheepskin-lined boots, and a long woolen muffler that she'd wrapped around her neck a dozen times. She still looked cold. Samantha had never really adjusted to the colder northern temperatures, and she was always cranky when the weather turned frigid.

"I love this weather," Kyle said cheerfully. "It really wakes you up."

"Oh, be quiet," Samantha snapped. "You've been telling me that all morning. What if I don't want to wake up?"

The grin slowly faded from Kyle's face. "Whoa, excuse me. I'll come back when you're acting human." Hitching his backpack over one shoulder, Kyle went up the steps and entered the school.

Samantha bit her lip. "Oh, shoot. This keeps happening. I don't know what I'm going to do."

"Why don't you try acting nice for a change?" Brittany suggested mildly.

Kim tossed her head. "Oh, you guys always make up, Sam—just chill out."

Samantha winced. "If I chill out any more, I'll turn into an ice cube."

Jeremy studied the white sky. "I just hope it doesn't snow again. I waxed my Porsche last weekend."

"Jeremy," Brittany said acidly, "do we have to discuss the state of your Porsche *every* morning?"

Samantha giggled as Kim became more visibly annoyed. Kim could complain about Jeremy for hours on end, but nobody else was allowed to. "I guess now that you're riding around in a Jaguar, Brittany, you think

Porsches are low rent," Kim said, letting Brittany know in an instant that she had found out about Brittany's reconciliation with Chip.

Brittany shrugged and decided to let it pass. "Maybe," she said airily. "Chip does have a gorgeous green Jaguar—the perfect car for a power couple."

"So the rumors are true—you did run back to him. How *are* things with Chip?" Samantha asked sarcastically.

"Fantastic," Brittany said, not giving in to Samantha either. "I saw him last night at the club for an early dinner." What she didn't add was that he'd bored her to tears with an endless account of a tennis game he'd played that afternoon, complete with a stroke-by-stroke replay of every serve and volley. Brittany had actually been relieved when his equally obnoxious friends turned up. Chip's friends always traveled in a pack, like wolves.

"And how are Chip's friends?" Kim asked.

"Oh, they're as much fun as always," Brittany gushed. "We're going to play doubles at the club this afternoon."

"You hate tennis," Samantha pointed out. "And you can't play."

"Chip's really helped my game," Brittany said brightly.

Kim and Samantha were studying her skeptically. Brittany would die before she'd admit they were right. There were just too many compensations for going out with Chip. The night before, they had sat at the best table in the country club dining room. That afternoon, the girl at the juice bar had taken Brittany's order ahead of three other people who were waiting. She had to admit she did like the special treatment.

If only Chip's friends treated her as well as the service people at the club. They still had a tendency to ignore her. Brittany knew that the girls were loyal to Missy, and the guys didn't think she was good enough for Chip.

Even though he was keeping up his casual act, Chip was obviously crazy about her. She had won him back, no doubt about it, but, Brittany wondered, could she win over his crowd? Even if she could, did she really want to?

As the end of the day approached, Nikki started to worry about her rehearsal with Tim. She knew some of her lines, so she wouldn't have to keep her nose buried in the script. Now she was nervous about the kiss between Lamont and Rita. She and Tim would have to rehearse it sooner or later. Would Tim actually kiss her? she wondered. Did she want him to?

When the last bell rang, Nikki got her books and coat and slowly headed toward the auditorium. On the way she saw Calvin at his locker. Nikki said a quick hello as she passed.

"Nikki, do you have a minute?" Calvin

asked, stopping her with a hand on her shoulder. His usually friendly green eyes were worried.

"Sure, Cal," Nikki said. "What's up?"

"It's Robin," Calvin said. "She told me she did her act for you last night."

"Yes," Nikki said reluctantly. "She did."

"Well, she ran through it for me, too," Cal said in a low tone. "What did you think, Nikki?"

"Well," Nikki said slowly, "I think Robin worked out a really good dance routine. And she has a lot of guts. She——"

"She stinks," Calvin blurted out. "Instead of detention, the official school punishment should be having to listen to Robin sing."

Nikki couldn't help laughing. "I know," she agreed, relieved that she and Cal had the same opinion. "But what are we going to do? She thinks she's great."

"That's the thing, Nikki," Calvin said nervously. "I can't tell Robin she's terrible. We'd probably get into a huge fight, and things have been terrific with us lately. Besides, I just can't hurt her like that."

"I see," Nikki said. She knew what was coming.

"But *you* could tell her," Calvin said. "You're so tactful, Nikki. And if the word came from you, Robin might accept it. You're a pro."

"I wouldn't say that," Nikki protested. But she knew Calvin was right. It really was her place to give Robin the bad news. She should have been more honest in the first place. She sighed in agreement. "I'll do it, Cal. I've been trying to think of the right words."

"How about, 'you stink'?" Calvin said with a shrug. "That should get the point across."

Nikki laughed. "You'd better stick with chemistry, Cal. Don't become an entertainment critic."

"Don't worry," Calvin said, shaking his head. "I don't have the nerve for it."

And I do? Nikki thought worriedly as she hurried away. It seemed as though lately she was bouncing from one unpleasant situation to another. With Gillian, Tim, and Robin, she'd need a rest cure after this week was over!

The day had started out great, but Karen's optimism had taken a nosedive by the time it was over. Ben had sat at Emily's table for lunch again. He seemed to have been heading for Karen, but Emily had waved him over. The only satisfaction Karen got was when Emily happened to pass her in the hall that afternoon. The blond beauty nodded a cool hello, and Karen completely ignored her.

The strain was getting to her, for sure. She'd probably flunked her chemistry quiz, and she'd had to avoid DeeDee Smith all day. Karen knew DeeDee wanted to ask her about the assignment that was due for the paper. She should have been researching photos that afternoon instead of shopping with Ellen.

Karen practically staggered out of her last class when the final bell rang. Eating only yogurt or cottage cheese for lunch every day was making her awfully light-headed. She was supposed to meet Ellen outside by the front steps. But first, Karen had to check something out.

She retrieved her coat from her locker and headed down the hallway. Ahead of her, she saw Ellen and Teresa waiting at the steps.

"Hi," Teresa said as Karen ran up. "You look like you're in a hurry."

"I'll meet you outside in two minutes, Ellen," Karen said.

"Okay," Ellen said dreamily.

"Look at Ellen," Teresa said to Karen. "Have you ever seen such a thrilled person? I'm going to have to tie a string to her so she won't float away."

Ellen grinned. "I just talked to Kevin," she told Karen. "He and his sister, Maggie, are going to ride with my family to the music competition on Saturday. Maggie is Suzanne's best friend, remember? Anyway, my mom and dad are taking us all out to dinner after the concert, to some really fancy place in Chicago."

"So Ellen will be with Kevin all day long," Teresa teased. "And all night, too, practically."

"That's nice," Karen said. She sneaked a peek at her watch.

"That reminds me. Do you want to sit with me on the bus Saturday, Karen?" Teresa asked. "I've been meaning to ask you, but I haven't seen much of you this week. And every time I call," she added, "you have to get off the phone in case Ben is trying to get through."

Karen decided to ignore Teresa's pointed comment. "I don't know if I'm going yet," she said.

Ellen seemed crestfallen, and Teresa looked at her incredulously. "Not going?" she blurted out. "But—"

"I don't know if Ben is going yet. I'm checking the list right now," Karen interrupted impatiently. She was wasting precious time. After buying a new dress, she had to check out some cookbooks from the library. Then she needed to stop at the card store and buy something funny and romantic to slip into Ben's locker the next morning.

"I've checked the list every day to see if Ben's name is on it," she continued. "I don't want to ask him straight out if he's going."

Ellen bit her lip. "I see," Teresa said tightly.

"So if you guys don't mind, I've got to rush. I'll meet you outside, Ellen. My mother let me borrow the car today, so we don't have to take the bus downtown. Is everything okay with your mom?"

"Fine," Ellen said softly. "She said she'd be delighted to help you out, Karen. She's expecting you."

Karen noticed Ellen didn't seem very enthusiastic about her shopping trip. If everything was cleared with Mrs. Ming, she wouldn't really need her friend. "You know, Ellen," she burst out, "you don't have to come with me if you don't want to. You'd probably rather go have a soda with Terry."

Ellen's gentle eyes were downcast, and she nodded. "Sure," she said. "I'll meet you outside, Terry. Good luck today, Karen." Ellen turned and headed down the hall.

Karen checked her watch again. "See you later, Terry," she said. "I've really got to—"

"You've really got to stay here and listen to me a minute," Teresa interrupted in a low, furious tone. "Just who do you think you are?"

Startled, Karen looked up. "What?"

"Are you so caught up in this obsession with Ben that you don't notice when you hurt people?" Teresa demanded. "Ellen was about to cry."

"Oh, don't exaggerate, Terry," Karen said impatiently. "Ellen's fine. She didn't want to go shopping, and I gave her an excuse so she wouldn't have to."

"No, she's not fine. And if you weren't being

so selfish you'd realize it. Haven't you thought about Ellen's feelings at all? Her sister is performing on Saturday—it's a big deal for the Mings and for Ellen. Don't you think she wants us at the concert? Even if the fabulous Ben Newhouse isn't going to attend?"

"Ellen didn't say anything—"

"She shouldn't have to! We should *want* to go, for her and her family. We're her best friends. Or at least one of us is. You're not acting like a best friend at all. Didn't you see how she was trying not to cry?"

Karen felt guilty. Teresa had never yelled at her before. "I'll apologize to Ellen, Terry. I *am* sorry. But I don't have time right this minute. I've got a million things to take care of."

"Fine," Teresa said shortly. "Go ahead. But I can save you a few precious seconds. I looked at the list today. Ben *is* going."

"Oh," Karen said. "Well, then, the problem is solved. I'll see Suzanne's performance. All right? I'll sign up right now." With a nervous smile, Karen turned away.

"If you want to find his name," Teresa shouted after her, "it's right under Emily Van Patten's!"

9

"I hate you!" Nikki shouted. "You are a piece of slime that was dredged up from a swamp! You are an oil slick off Santa Barbara! And this is the worst plate of spaghetti I've ever eaten!" Nikki picked up the plastic plate Tim had borrowed from the cafeteria. She aimed it at him and threw.

The plate hit Tim harmlessly in the chest, just as they'd rehearsed. It bounced to the wooden stage, and the sound echoed once in the empty auditorium.

"You don't mean it," Tim said, taking a step toward her. "Passion doesn't exist in a vacuum, Rita."

"Why are we talking about housekeeping, Lamont?" Nikki snarled. "You're the biggest slob in the world. You think a vacuum is something to hang your dirty underwear on.''

Tim reached her side. "I'm not talking about housekeeping, Rita," he said, his voice throaty now. "I'm talking about passion.''

Nikki tilted her head back as Tim walked up so close that her nose was touching his chin. For a moment she'd really been Rita. But suddenly, as Tim drew near her, she'd turned back into Nikki again. And Nikki was just as nervous and scared as Rita was.

Tim grabbed her by the forearms. He dipped his head. Mesmerized, Nikki watched his mouth come closer and closer. Finally his lips closed on hers.

Nikki's head swam as the memory of hundreds of other kisses Tim had given her merged with the feel of his warm lips against hers again. His kiss was soft and insistent at the same time. His arms slid around her, and he clasped her to him as if any space between them was too much.

Then Tim broke the kiss and looked deep into her eyes. Nikki felt just a little dizzy.

Tim stepped back. "Okay," he said crisply. "I think we're making progress here." He dropped his arms and picked up her hand. "Maybe, though, you should put this hand on my neck. The audience will see it, and it's a nice intimate gesture. It will show that, despite her attraction to Lamont, Rita does trust him. The neck is a vulnerable area.''

"Right," Nikki said dazedly. Tim was acting so professional! Hadn't he been affected by the kiss at all?

"Listen, while I think of it, I need to talk to you about something," Tim said. "I saw in one of the Chicago papers that the Windy City Repertory Company is putting on a revival of *The Blue Moon Luncheonette*. It's playing this Saturday. We could go after the music competition. I talked to Mrs. Burns about it. She said if four other people from the drama club were interested, she'd chaperon. Would you like to go, Nikki? It'd be great for us to see the play in performance."

"Sure," Nikki said slowly. Now she'd *have* to go to Chicago and see Gillian. How could she say no to Tim?

"Great! I'll work out the details."

"Is Lara going?" Nikki asked. Now, why had she asked that? She didn't care one way or another, really.

"I haven't told her about it yet," Tim said coolly. He moved back to his former position. "Okay, let's take the scene again from where you first pick up the plate. We'll block the kiss again. But this time I don't think we have to rehearse it. We'll just do it at the audition."

"Good idea," Nikki said weakly. The mere thought of kissing Tim again made her feel confused. She stooped to pick up the plastic plate and returned to her position. She stared down at the plate and thought of Tim's strong fingers on her arms and the way he had held her so close. Could he have squeezed all the air out of her lungs? Was that why she felt so breathless?

"Nikki?" Tim prodded. "Do you need a minute to prepare?"

A minute? She needed a lot more time than that. "Thanks," she said weakly. She closed her eyes, trying to summon up Rita's anger again. But she couldn't. All her concentration had flown out the window. Right then none of her emotions were very clear. What was happening to her?

Karen found the dress immediately. It was emerald green silk with a plain neckline in front but a deep, sexy V in the back. The skirt clung to her hips and legs and ended above her knees. Best of all, her dressy black pumps would do fine. She'd been afraid she'd have to buy shoes, too.

Mrs. Ming tactfully suggested that the dress might be a bit too old for her, but Karen had to have it. She didn't even care that the dress used up every penny of the money her mother had given her, as well as her allowance for the next two weeks. She was skipping lunches, anyway, and Ben loved her in green.

She paid cash for the dress without even blinking and took the precious package in its distinctive gray Maison de Mode dress bag. She felt so sophisticated as she walked down the street. If only Emily could see her now!

The glow from her shopping expedition lasted through the rest of the afternoon. That night Karen pored over cookbooks instead of textbooks. Every half hour or so she couldn't help but touch the cool fabric of the dress. Then she returned to her desk to scrawl another menu, tear up the paper, and try again. Finally she decided on chicken Dijon, potatoes Anna, string beans, rolls, and salad. For dessert, she would bake her mother's famous dense chocolate cake. She'd leave out the walnuts, of course.

Thursday morning Karen slipped the romantic card into Ben's locker. She managed to talk to him for fifteen minutes at lunch before he sat down to eat with Lacey Dupree. He had junior class business to attend to with Lacey, he said. At least he wasn't sitting with Emily—and he smiled at Karen and said he couldn't wait for Friday night.

After school Karen hurried to the *Record* meeting DeeDee Smith had called that day for writers and editors. It was annoying, but Karen had to attend. DeeDee told her in no uncertain terms that everybody had to be there. Karen hoped the meeting wouldn't last long. She knew Ben had a short committee conference, so she hoped to catch him afterward in the parking lot. If Ben didn't ask her to go for a soda, she'd do the grocery shopping right after the meeting. Then Friday she could devote the afternoon to preparing the meal and turning herself into the gorgeous, sophisticated creature of Ben's dreams.

"Attention, people," DeeDee called. She looked around the *Record* office, a deep frown creasing her pretty face. The staff members looked up uneasily.

Brittany almost groaned out loud. DeeDee obviously had some kind of gripe to get off her chest, and Brittany knew Chip would be waiting outside. Brittany wasn't thrilled about seeing him, but she also didn't want to waste time here. She'd handed in her profile on Gillian St. James that morning. It was a terrific piece, and Brittany knew DeeDee would love it.

Well, on second thought, Chip could wait, Brittany thought tiredly. She wasn't anxious to spend yet another afternoon at the country club. Chip absolutely refused to go to the Pizza Palace or to Leon's. He didn't want to be seen in any River Heights High hangouts. He was such a bore!

DeeDee smacked a pile of papers against the palm of one hand. She looked *very* unhappy, Brittany thought uneasily. She had a feeling the staff was in for one of DeeDee's famous tirades. Mr. Green, the faculty adviser, stood behind her, his arms crossed. At least Brittany wasn't at fault this time.

"I am extremely disappointed in each and every member of this staff," DeeDee said in a clear voice that vibrated with barely controlled fury. "Just because we've put out a couple of decent issues, you think you can slide. Well, your sliding days are over!" To punctuate the remark, DeeDee threw the pile of papers in the garbage can. Somebody in the back gasped.

"That was the material I received for our next issue," DeeDee said disdainfully. "And *that* is where it belongs." She turned to Kevin Hoffman, who wrote a humor column. "Do you really think we need to read *another* exposé of cafeteria food, Kevin? That was a lazy piece of writing."

"Sorry, DeeDee," Kevin said with his lopsided grin. "I recently developed a social life."

DeeDee held his gaze until Kevin's grin faded. "Not good enough, Kevin," she said crisply. "I don't care if you're busy. I don't care if you're happy. I don't care if you're *miserable.* I still expect you to be funny." She turned to Karen Jacobs. "I asked you days ago to research photos on that 'Fifty Years Ago at River Heights High' story, Karen. What's going on?"

A deep blush spread over Karen's face. "I forgot, DeeDee. I've been busy. I'm sorry."

"You *forgot?*" DeeDee shook her head.

"Well," she said sarcastically, "maybe you can squeeze us in sometime soon, Karen."

Serves Karen right, Brittany crowed inwardly. She loved to see Karen get blasted by DeeDee. Usually Karen was the editor-in-chief's pet. It looked as if Ben Newhouse's drooling over Emily Van Patten was interfering with Karen's meticulous work habits. The girl was obviously spending more time on her hair than on her work. The best thing, Brittany thought smugly as DeeDee lit into Dave Reed, the music critic, was that all Karen's efforts would be for nothing. What guy would be blind enough to choose drab Karen Jacobs over super-model Emily Van Patten?

This was turning out to be a fun meeting after all. It was just delicious to see everyone get yelled at while she, Brittany, was smelling like a rose. She leaned back in her chair and studied her red cowboy boots. She couldn't wait to see Chip's face when he saw them. Brittany had to admit she got a kick out of irritating him. She could tell that he was dying to ask why she didn't wear his pearls. He'd even suggested that a "necklace" would complement an outfit she had on. It had been really hard for her not to burst out laughing.

"And as for you, Brittany," DeeDee rapped out. Brittany looked up, startled. Why did DeeDee sound so annoyed?

"Would you mind telling me," DeeDee asked icily, "why you did a profile on someone who isn't connected in any way with River Heights High?"

"She's the girlfriend of a student here," Brittany said with a shrug.

"Old girlfriend," Karen interjected.

Brittany shot Karen an evil look. "She's from England, which is really interesting. And she's in the Young Players Music Competition," she elaborated to DeeDee. "I think that's important."

"It is," DeeDee said coolly. "But we had assigned you a piece on Suzanne Ming. She is one of our own students and is also in the competition. Suzanne Ming is only a freshman, so her being in the contest is an even greater accomplishment. I think that's more important news, don't you?"

Suzanne Ming was a nobody, and she'd be a totally boring interview. DeeDee could show a real lack of imagination sometimes. Brittany would have made a much better editor-in-chief. "I was planning to do the article on Suzanne for the following issue," Brittany said, bluffing.

"It'll be old news by then, Brittany. Get on it right now. I want to see a revised column Monday, with an account of the competition itself." DeeDee returned her attention to the group. "About the only staff member I'm not completely disgusted with is Nikki Masters. She went out on her own and got some fabulous shots of Moon Lake yesterday after the snow.

Then she developed the prints during her lunch hour today. You all could take lessons from that kind of initiative. Now get moving, people, and turn in some pieces we can be proud of.''

Great, Brittany fumed as she stormed out of the office. The Barbie doll got all the credit, as usual. Nothing in life was fair.

Karen Jacobs hurried ahead of her, her silly, newly waved hair flying. She pushed open the front doors ahead of Brittany, letting them almost slam back in Brittany's face.

Sourly, Brittany stepped outside. She was just in time to see Karen notice Emily Van Patten getting into Ben's Toyota. Karen looked as though she was about to burst into tears. Brittany cheered up immediately.

"Brittany! Over here!" Chip was waving at her from his Jaguar. He was parked in the no-parking zone directly in front of the walk so that Brittany's dainty feet wouldn't have to touch a particle of slush.

She tossed her head and swept past Karen, who was slumped against the school building. As she headed for the gleaming sports car, Brittany revised her former opinion. Not *everything* in life was unfair. Sometimes there was justice in the world after all.

After school on Friday Nikki took Robin home with her. Lacey would join them later, since she was stopping by Rick's house first. Robin had decided to try another practice performance, this time for both her best friends. As soon as they reached Nikki's bedroom, Robin changed into a black leotard and a big white shirt. Nikki was dreading the repeat performance. She still hadn't been able to tell Robin the whole truth about her singing.

She and Robin were just opening their cans of soda when Lacey burst into Nikki's bedroom. Her usually pale face was red, and she tore off her jacket and threw it on the floor.

"Something wrong, Lacey?" Nikki asked mildly.

"Nothing," Lacey said, stomping over to Nikki's bed and sitting on the edge of it. She crossed her legs and jiggled her foot. "What's new with you guys?"

Nikki and Robin exchanged glances.

"Come on, kiddo," Robin said. "Talk."

Lacey sighed. "I thought when Rick got better that we'd never have another fight. Boy, was I wrong. The accident didn't bring us closer together at all."

"What do you mean?" Nikki asked, concerned.

"Rick's almost fully recovered, you know. He just has to go to physical therapy twice a week for his left knee." Lacey hesitated.

"And?" Robin prompted.

"And there's this girl there. Her name is Katie Fox. She was in a car accident, and she has to have physical therapy for her leg." Lacey stopped again.

"So?" Nikki asked. "Do you think Rick has a crush on her or something?"

Lacey's eyes filled with tears. "I don't know," she whispered. "He says he doesn't. But he talks about her all the time. And he's always staying late at the hospital. He's so moody, too! When I try to talk to him, he says I can't understand how he feels. He says that only someone who's been in a bad accident can understand."

"Someone like Katie Fox," Robin guessed.

Lacey nodded. "I guess it's good for him to

have a friend he can talk to," she said, trying to grin through her tears. "But I don't want that friend to be a cute girl!"

"No way," Robin agreed.

"I know exactly how you feel," Nikki said wryly.

Lacey wiped her tears away with a determined hand. "I'll just have to get hold of myself, that's all. Rick will be coming back to school soon, and things will get back to normal then." She sighed. "I hope so, anyway. By the way, Nikki, what's going on with you and Niles?" Lacey looked eager to change the subject.

"Nothing," Nikki said. "We're going out tonight."

"Great!" Lacey said.

"With Gillian," Nikki added shortly.

"Oh. Well, at least you're going out together," Lacey said philosophically.

"Niles said Gillian wants some authentic American diner food, so we're going to this place called Slim and Shorty's Good Eats Café. It's way over by the river."

"Never heard of it," Lacey said.

"I have," Robin said. "There was a review in the paper last week. It's not much on atmosphere, but it's supposed to have the best chili in town."

Nikki shrugged. "I'm not exactly looking forward to it, but what can I do?" She hoped they'd keep talking about dinner. The longer they did, the longer she could put off having to hear Robin sing.

As if she'd read Nikki's mind, Robin jumped up. "Lacey will have to leave for work soon, so we'd better get this show on the road." She directed Lacey into the armchair and Nikki into the desk chair.

Her finger poised over the tape player, Robin looked at them solemnly. "Ready?"

Lacey and Nikki nodded.

Robin pushed the play button, and the music to "You're a Big Fat Zero, but I Really Like Your Face" began. Robin started her dance steps, and Lacey sat up in pleasure, a broad smile on her face. The smile stayed on through the opening bars. Then Robin began to sing.

Slowly Lacey's delighted smile became more and more strained. Soon it appeared to have been plastered onto her face. Her light blue eyes held a look of horror. She was pressed back against the cushions of the chair as though she wanted to get as far away from Robin as possible.

Finally the music ended. Lacey gave a quick, horrified glance at Nikki.

"Great, Rob," she said, springing up. "You're a terrific dancer. Really terrific. I had no idea. Really."

"Thanks, Lacey." Robin wiped a bit of perspiration off her forehead. "How did you like my singing?"

"I—I was overwhelmed," Lacey stammered. She looked at Nikki's bedside digital clock. "And I'm late. Lenny will kill me. I'll talk to you guys tomorrow. 'Bye."

Lacey grabbed her jacket and dashed out of the room. Robin beamed at Nikki. "She really liked my singing," she said.

Nikki took a deep breath. It was now or never. The tryouts were Monday afternoon. "Robin, I need to talk to you about your act," she said.

Robin gave a professional-looking nod. She sat in the chair next to Nikki and threw her legs over the arm so she could face her. "Some pointers? Great. Shoot."

Nikki closed her eyes. "Robin, you can't sing," she said quickly. She opened her eyes again and peeked at her friend.

Robin frowned. "What do you mean? Do you mean I shouldn't sing for the contest for some reason—like a lot of other people are auditioning as singers?"

Nikki shook her head.

Slowly the meaning of Nikki's comment began to dawn on Robin. "Wait a second. Do you mean I *can't sing?*" she wailed incredulously.

Nikki nodded. "You can't carry a tune," she said in a small voice. "You try hard, and you have a lot of energy, but . . ." Nikki let her voice trail off. She didn't know what else to say.

Robin sprang up, her face red. "Thanks a lot,

Nikki," she said. Tears were standing in her big dark eyes. "Some friend you are. You're telling me I'm completely untalented, right?"

"No," Nikki assured her. "I'm just saying—"

"I can't believe this," Robin interrupted. "Why didn't you tell me before?"

"You didn't give me a chance," Nikki said.

Robin put her hands on her hips. "Oh, you mean I didn't give you a chance at lunch or before school or after school? When *exactly* didn't I give you a chance, Nikki?"

"Okay," Nikki admitted. "I guess I was afraid you'd get angry."

"Me, get angry? Thanks a lot!" Robin stormed. "I'm much too professional to get angry!" She stamped her foot. "So there!"

Nikki bit her lip. She didn't want to hurt Robin's feelings, but it was kind of funny to hear Robin practically scream at her that she wasn't a bit angry.

Robin bit her lip, too. Then she burst out laughing. Nikki laughed in relief as Robin flung herself on the floor in a dramatic pose.

"Okay, maybe I *was* angry," she said. "I worked so hard! Now you're telling me that I stink."

"No, I'm not," Nikki said quickly. "If you'd just let me get a word in. I meant what I said about your dancing. I think it's great, honestly."

Robin sniffed. "Cal and Lacey liked my

dancing, too. They didn't say anything about my singing, though. Come to think of it, Cal looked a little queasy. He said he'd eaten too many french fries at Leon's. And Lacey didn't have to be at work for another half hour at least." Robin grimaced. "I guess you're a true friend, Nikki. I'm sorry I got mad."

"It's okay," Nikki said.

"But, Nikki, what am I going to do now?" Robin said, turning over and resting her chin in her hands. "I really wanted to do this. I had so much fun thinking up the routine! I even fantasized about winning a prize. It was the best daydream I ever had," she concluded mournfully.

Nikki stared thoughtfully at Robin's shapely legs. It was a shame that Robin couldn't sing. Suddenly Nikki sat up and snapped her fingers.

"I've got it! Fisher, you're still going to try out."

"And make a fool of myself?" Robin shook her head. "No way."

"No, silly." Nikki leaned forward eagerly. "You're not going to sing. You're going to lip-synch!"

Karen looked at the clock again. Preparing this dinner had been more time-consuming than she'd expected. She'd had to run to the store twice for last-minute items, and at four o'clock she'd suddenly remembered flowers. What was a romantic dinner without flowers?

She should have bought an elegant bouquet at Blooms, but she had to settle for some irises from the grocery store. At least she found some lilac-colored candles to match. Now she was really in debt to her mother. She'd be doing chores through college to pay for this night.

By four-thirty she'd made the marinade for the chicken and was setting the table. Then she washed all the expensive salad greens. Finally, she raced upstairs to bathe in her mother's expensive designer bath oil. She washed her hair for the second time that day and twisted it into curlers.

Back downstairs in her robe, Karen started the preparation for the complicated potatoes Anna. This would be the most impressive dish on the table. The picture in the cookbook showed a bubbling golden brown casserole. Her mother even had the copper dish that was absolutely essential. Karen sliced the potatoes and heated the butter, then carefully added the potatoes in layers along with more butter, grated onion, and Parmesan cheese. It seemed to take forever.

"Whoever Anna was, I hate her," Karen muttered as she worked frantically.

Finally the dish was ready to be baked. Karen put it aside until later. Then she started work on the dense chocolate cake. She burned the first batch of butter, and in her haste dropped the bag of flour on the floor. When her mother came downstairs, Karen was standing in a pile of flour with tears running down her face.

"Ben will be here in less than an hour," she sobbed. "I haven't even done my hair yet!"

Her mother frowned in concern. "Oh, honey, I don't know why you chose such a complicated menu. Maybe you should have made the dessert last night."

Karen burst into fresh sobs. Her mother was right, as usual. The dinner would be a fiasco!

Mrs. Jacobs patted her shoulder sympathetically. "I'm sorry, sweetie. I'm sure the dinner will be fabulous." She reached for an apron and quickly tied it around her waist. "I have about a half hour before your father and I have to leave. Why don't you let me make the cake?"

Karen nodded tearfully. "Thanks, Mom. Everything has to be perfect."

Her mother frowned slightly. "No, it doesn't. Ben will love you no matter what. Now, you go on upstairs and get yourself fixed up. Ben won't mind if you're running a little behind."

"I guess not," Karen sniffed. But she wouldn't run behind, she resolved. She'd pull this dinner together, or else!

11 ～～

A car horn honked outside the Tate house at ten minutes past seven that evening. Brittany sighed and grabbed her coat and purse. Now that she and Chip were a couple, he rarely bothered to come to the door.

Mr. Tate came out of the living room, holding his newspaper and frowning. "Why doesn't that Chip person come to the door for you, Brittany?"

Brittany slipped into her coat. "We're late, Dad," she explained. "And I wish you wouldn't call him 'that Chip person.' You can just call him Chip, you know."

Tamara, Brittany's thirteen-year-old sister, stuck her head out of the living room. "Dad calls the Snob 'that Chip person' because he can't stand him, Britty. Nobody but you can stand him."

Brittany stuck her tongue out at Tamara. It was a childish thing to do, but her sister could be extremely annoying. "Good night, everyone," she said. "Don't wait up."

"Try to come home early tonight, Brittany," her father said with a sigh. As he headed back to the living room, she heard him mumble, "I don't want you to stay out late with that Chip person."

Brittany hurried down the front walk to Chip's car. Seeing that Jaguar was enough to put her back into a good mood. She slid into the palomino-colored leather seat and kissed Chip on the cheek. "I wish you'd come to the door," she said, drawing back with a tiny pout. "My dad had a fit when you blew the horn."

"Sorry. We're late," Chip said, putting the car into gear.

"Did you make reservations somewhere?" Brittany asked hopefully. Like Le Saint-Tropez, the fancy French restaurant, she hoped.

"I told the gang we'd meet them at the club," Chip said. "Tad reserved the big table in the dining room." He reached over and took her hand.

Brittany wanted to scream. She'd never dreamed she could get so bored at the country club. She loved going there, of course, but not as a steady diet! And why did they always have to hang out with Chip's crowd? She was getting sick of him and them, real fast. Brittany snatched her hand away and stared stonily out the window.

"What's up?" Chip asked flippantly. "Are we a little angry because I didn't come to the door like Prince Charming?"

"Yes, we are," Brittany snapped. "We are also not crazy about going to the club on every single date."

"You want a change of scenery. I can deal with that," Chip said smoothly.

Brittany softened a bit. "I wouldn't mind trying a new restaurant," she hinted. She reached over and slipped her hand into Chip's again.

Chip raised her hand to his lips and kissed it. "Your wish is my command," he said lightly. "We'll go somewhere very special tonight."

Brittany smiled and settled back into the soft leather seat. She was wearing her dressy white wool trousers with a creamy satin blouse. She'd fit in anywhere, even Le Saint-Tropez. She'd never been there, but Kim had. She couldn't wait to tell Kim she'd gone there. She'd call her first thing the next morning.

Brittany jumped when Chip snapped his fingers. "I've got it! I know where we can go."

"Where?" Brittany asked hopefully.

"I just saw a review of a new place by the river," Chip said. "It's out in the middle of absolutely nowhere, but the food is supposed to be very cool. It's called Slim and Shorty's Good Eats Café. Isn't that a hoot?"

A real hoot, Brittany thought desperately. She'd been a waitress at Slim and Shorty's just a couple of months earlier! "It sounds like a dive," she said to Chip.

"Where's your sense of adventure?" Chip asked. "You wanted to try someplace new." He made the turn toward the country club. "Let's just pick up the gang," he said. "They'll flip."

Brittany's heart sank. Wait until Shorty, the hulking six-foot-five owner in the greasy white apron, saw her. She'd get a big hello from him and his partner, the pudgy, loud-mouthed Slim. Everyone would know that she'd actually been a waitress in that grease pit!

She was quiet as they rounded up Tad, Bob, Wesley, Dee, and Trudy, and the caravan of cars headed for the river. She'd have to do some fast thinking, that was for sure.

As soon as Chip pulled up in the lunar landscape that was the café parking lot, Brittany sprang out of the car. "I'll just run ahead and get us a good table," she flung at Chip as she slammed the door.

She nearly twisted an ankle in a pothole, but she was able to run ahead and beg Shorty not to recognize her. Shorty was a good guy—he didn't even ask her why. He just winked and nodded. The rest of the group came in then, and Shorty led them to a table in the rear. He winked at Brittany after they were seated.

"You seem to have a new admirer," Chip observed when Shorty left. "I'd tell the hulk to chill out, but he's awfully, uh, large."

"Just ignore him," Brittany said nervously.

Trudy gave an exaggerated sigh. "Too bad Missy couldn't make it," she said with a significant glance at Brittany.

"Too bad," Brittany replied sweetly.

"We definitely need another girl," Wesley said. "Poor Bob here is lonely."

Bob blushed. "Shut up, Wesley," he snapped.

Chip turned to Brittany. "Maybe you could get that new friend of yours, Gillian St. James, to meet us. She's a knockout."

"Oh, no," Brittany blurted out before she could think. "She couldn't possibly make it."

Trudy looked at her suspiciously. "How do you know, Brittany?" she asked. "Maybe you should call her, anyway."

"Or maybe you're not such good friends after all." Dee smirked.

If those two thought they could trap her so easily, they didn't know Brittany Tate. "She never goes out the night before a performance," Brittany said glibly.

"You seem to know her pretty well," Bob said.

"Yes, we really hit it off," Brittany gushed. "She's invited me to stay at Parkhurst this summer. It's her family's estate, you know. It even has a ghost. I just can't wait! Of course, we'll probably spend some time in the center of London, too. The St. Jameses have a darling flat there." Thank goodness Gillian was returning to England soon. Brittany could always say the trip had been postponed.

"London is a blast," Chip said. "I was there last summer. And if Gillian is any indication, I'd say it's time to check out the girls—or birds, as they say over there—one more time."

Chip, Tad, Wesley, and Bob all guffawed. Brittany inched away from Chip, annoyed. For such a wealthy guy, Chip had no class.

"Whoa," Tad said suddenly. "Speak of the devil—or should I say the angel. Isn't that Gillian St. James?"

Oh, no! With a sinking heart, Brittany turned. Gillian, Niles, and Nikki were entering Slim and Shorty's. Who would have thought they'd come to this dump? Brittany wanted to hide under the table.

Trudy tapped the table with a long polished fingernail. "Funny to see her here," she said. "I mean, this *is* the night before her performance."

"Why don't you wave her over?" Dee suggested meanly. "I want to ask Gillian more about that fabulous estate you're going to visit."

Brittany squirmed on the vinyl seat of the booth. The *tap-tap* of Trudy's fingernail seemed to echo the sound of a deadly trap snapping closed. Had she been caught?

The doorbell rang while Karen was desperately trying to comb out the curls in her hair. That gel she had applied lavishly must have actually been rubber cement. It had bonded her hair into tiny corkscrew curls all over her head.

The bell rang again. Karen gave herself another look in the mirror. She wanted to burst into tears, but she knew that would ruin her makeup. At least she could smell the fragrant chicken baking downstairs. Even if she looked like Shirley Temple, her meal would be worthy of a chef like Julia Child.

Quickly she teetered down the hall toward the stairs. The skirt was too tight for her legs to move freely, and she wasn't used to wearing heels. She had to hang on to the banister for dear life. When her feet hit the polished hardwood floor of the entrance hall, she started to slide. Her palms slapped against the front door and she hugged it for dear life. Finally she smoothed her hair, put a warm smile on her face, and opened the door.

"Hi," Ben said. "I hope I'm not—" He looked at Karen, his mouth open in surprise. "Hey, what happened to your hair?"

Karen felt like punching him. "I thought you liked it in curls," she said in a honeyed tone of voice.

Ben nodded. "Sure, but tonight it kind of looks like a headful of tiny Slinky toys."

Karen gave a little laugh, even though she wanted to slug him. "Come on in, Ben," she trilled. "Let me have your jacket."

Ben handed her his corduroy jacket. He was dressed in jeans and a white shirt under a navy sweater. He was even wearing running shoes. Karen felt kind of silly in her expensive dress and high-heeled pumps. Couldn't Ben have dressed up a little bit?

He seemed to notice her emerald silk dress for the first time. "Gosh," he said, "I didn't know this was a formal occasion. I would have worn a tie."

"Don't be silly," Karen said, gritting her teeth. "I want you to be comfortable."

Ben sniffed the air appreciatively. "Dinner smells great."

Karen led the way into the living room. While they sipped tomato juice garnished with paper-thin slices of lemon, she questioned Ben about his school activities, his schoolwork, his family, and his favorite professional football team. She'd written out a list of topics that would interest him. She managed to keep her expression vivacious and interested, even while she mentally went over her checklist in search of the next topic.

Suddenly Karen realized that they'd been sitting and talking for almost a half hour. Shouldn't the oven buzzer have gone off?

"Excuse me for one little second," she said sweetly. She ran to the kitchen. When she yanked open the oven door, she was glad to see that the chicken hadn't burned. But the potatoes Anna didn't have that golden brown color. In fact, Karen saw with dismay, they looked rather charred. Maybe she could scrape off the top before she brought the casserole to the table.

"Everything okay?" Ben yelled.

"Be right there," she sang out. Quickly she took out the chicken and potatoes and slid a pan of rolls into the oven. She'd cheated and used the kind that came in a tube, but Ben wouldn't know. The rolls would take ten minutes, and while they were cooking she could dress the salad and make the potatoes look edible.

Instead of using bottled dressing, Karen had decided to make her mother's mustard vinaigrette. But now she couldn't find the recipe anywhere! She could have tucked it into one of the cookbooks when she was searching for recipes. But Karen had seen her mother make it many times. She couldn't mess it up.

Quickly she mixed oil and vinegar and mustard. What else? Tarragon, Karen remembered. The spices were over the stove. Karen hoisted herself up on the counter to reach for the herb. She heard something rip. It was her new dress. Oh, no! She wasn't used to wearing such a tight skirt.

Quickly, she grabbed the tarragon and scrambled back down. There was a long tear in the side seam. Now the skirt would flap around her legs instead of clinging to them seductively, but she didn't have time to worry about it. Karen dumped some tarragon into the dressing and went to work on the potatoes Anna. She sawed away at the charred top, picking off the black pieces. Soon the dish looked as though it had been blown up and reassembled.

"Need any help?" Ben called.

"No," Karen screeched. Then she carefully modulated her voice and called, "You can sit at the table, though. Dinner's ready."

She scurried into the dining room and lit the candles, burning her index finger in the process. She ran back into the kitchen and dumped the chicken into a fancy casserole dish. She slammed it on the table before her fingers burned. Then she ran back to the kitchen to check the rolls. They didn't look quite done, and she noticed that she'd switched off the oven after she took out the chicken. Well, the oven was still hot, so they were probably okay. Karen brought them to the table along with the salad.

"Looks delicious," Ben said warmly. Karen smiled briefly and ran back for the potatoes. Ben looked at them dubiously. "I'm sure they *taste* delicious."

Suddenly Karen remembered the string beans. She'd forgotten to cook them! Well, Ben would just have to make do with salad. She picked up her knife and fork to cut her chicken. Ben was already sawing away valiantly at his. It *was* a little hard to cut. As a matter of fact, she could have bought the chicken in a novelty store. It was like rubber.

"Delicious," Ben said around a mouthful, but he wasn't smiling.

Karen took a bite of potatoes. They tasted as burned as they looked. The rolls were barely cooked and were more like raw dough. Then she took a bite of salad. She began to choke on the overpowering vinegar, and Ben came over to pound her on the back.

Disaster! Everything was awful. Karen was so embarrassed she wanted to die. She'd wanted the meal to be romantic and elegant, but it was anything but. The worst part was that she was too nervous to make a joke about it. She was afraid she'd just burst into tears— and she had to stay upbeat!

Finally Ben put down his fork. "That was great, Karen. Thanks."

With a hopeful start, Karen suddenly re- membered dessert. Her mother had baked the dense chocolate cake, so it had to be good. Ben helped her gather the plates and silverware and take them to the kitchen. "Go back and sit down," she told him. "You're in for a real treat now."

"Can't wait," Ben said heartily.

Proudly Karen brought out the cake. It

smelled delicious, and when she cut into it, it looked absolutely perfect. She placed a generous slice on Ben's plate.

Even Ben seemed cheered. He took a big forkful and chewed happily. Then, suddenly, his expression changed.

"What?" Karen asked frantically. "What is it?"

Ben swallowed with difficulty. He turned woeful brown eyes on Karen. "Walnuts," he said.

12

Brittany got a reprieve when Gillian went to the ladies' room. But finally, when Trudy urged her for the fourth time, Brittany had to catch Gillian's eye and beckon her over.

Gillian looked smashing as she came toward Brittany. She was wearing a shirt in a bright orange pattern, the same black mini she'd worn the other day, and black suspenders.

"Hello, Brittany," Gillian said as she came up. "I didn't see you when we arrived."

Quickly Brittany introduced her to Chip and his pack. Everyone said hello, and Dee looked at Trudy, then back at Gillian. "Brittany's been telling us all about Parkhurst," she said.

"Has she?" Gillian said politely. "It's an old drafty pile of stone, really."

"We hear you have a ghost," Bob said.

"Yes, old Willy," Gillian said, laughing.

Dee smiled tightly. "Brittany will have to be careful," she said.

Gillian's expression was puzzled.

"You'll have to take plenty of sweaters, Brittany," Trudy added.

Gillian frowned before giving a quick glance at Brittany. Brittany turned her head away, unable to face Gillian's puzzled green eyes.

Dee seemed to take heart from Gillian's confusion. "Brittany's been telling us about your kind invitation to visit you next summer. She can't wait." She sat back, a smug expression on her face.

"Yes," Trudy said. "It will be a treat for her. I mean," she went on with an affected laugh, *"we've* been to Europe, of course. But Brittany, well, she usually spends her summers in River Heights, if you know what I mean."

Dee smiled conspiratorially at Gillian, and the friendly grin instantly left the English girl's face. Her adorable nose wrinkled, as though she'd smelled something unpleasant.

Brittany wanted to die. This was it. Gillian had summed up the situation, and now Brittany would be exposed as a liar and a fraud in front of everybody. She felt all the color drain from her face, and she knew Chip's eyes were on her. Brittany could only stare at her place mat as if it were the most fascinating thing in the world.

Suddenly Gillian flashed Brittany a dazzling grin. "Was it summer? I hoped you might come during your spring vacation, Brittany," she said. "I was confused for a moment. I guess it's because I can't wait, either. You know," she confided to the table, "Brittany has been such a love. She's proof that some Americans really have class. So many don't," she added with a pointed glance at Trudy and Dee. Trudy pressed her thin lips together, and Dee smoothed her bangs self-consciously.

"How true," Brittany agreed, straightening.

"It was nice meeting you all," Gillian concluded brightly. "Brittany, don't you forget to call me!"

Brittany waved and smiled. "I won't!" she trilled. She'd lucked out! Gillian had saved her neck. Trudy and Dee had been so mean that they'd foiled their own plot. The distaste on Gillian's face had been for those two goons, not for Brittany.

"Shall we order?" she asked, cheerfully picking up the menu.

Dee frowned. "I don't see a decent salad on this menu," she complained.

"I'm sure they have iceberg lettuce smothered in mayonnaise," Trudy said with a shudder.

"All right, I give up," Tad said nastily. "Next time we'll just eat at the club."

"I'm with you, old man," Chip said.

Brittany looked despairingly from one sulky face to another. She *had* been saved, it was true. But saved for what? Slow death by boredom.

Karen closed the front door on Ben. His footsteps headed toward the driveway for his car. A sob broke loose, and Karen leaned her head against the door and cried her heart out.

It wasn't that she had overdressed and looked like a fool. It wasn't that she had a headful of Slinky toys for hair. It wasn't even that the food was awful or that Ben had already begun to break out in spots from the walnuts in the cake.

It was that, normally, she and Ben would have had a good laugh over all these things. But Ben had hardly said a word. Things between them were completely spoiled.

It was all her fault! Karen turned away from the door and savagely kicked off her high heels. At this time the night before, she had been imagining a different scene. The romantic dinner over, she and Ben would curl up on the living room couch. Karen would bring in the candles from the table, and they would kiss and be close, just the way they used to be. But the reality had been much different from the fantasy. After dinner Ben couldn't wait to run out the door.

Karen reached behind her to tug down her

zipper. It stuck. She yanked at it, and she heard the material tear.

That did it! Karen practically tore off the dress and crumpled it into a ball. She'd wasted tons of money on that dress. Teresa was furious with her. She'd hurt Ellen's feelings, and DeeDee was disappointed in her. All for nothing! She was tired of acting like a sweet, perfect person to Ben while she messed up the rest of her life.

Suddenly Karen felt disgusted with herself. She would miss Ben, sure. But if he didn't like her the way she was, too bad. He just wasn't worth all this trouble!

Clutching the dress, Karen ran upstairs. She seized her oldest pair of jeans and pulled them on, along with a soft gray sweater. She gathered her hair into a high ponytail. Ellen and Teresa had said they were going out that night. She'd look for them at the Loft first. And if they weren't there, she'd have a cheeseburger and fries by herself. Now that she was acting like a normal person again, Karen realized she was starving.

Luckily she had her mom's car. Karen felt better as she drove to the Loft. She hurried inside, but didn't see Teresa and Ellen. Well, she'd wolf down a burger and then call to see if they were home yet.

Karen ordered a cheeseburger deluxe and a double serving of fries. When the food arrived, it smelled heavenly. When was the last time she'd eaten real food? All she needed now was some mustard. Karen glanced around, but all the tables around her had only ketchup. She knelt on the seat of her booth and peeked over the partition. Only the top of a blond head was visible. The lone diner was bent over a fashion magazine.

There was a jar of mustard at the end of the table. "Excuse me," Karen said. "Can I borrow your mustard?"

"Sure." The occupant of the table looked up. Her long-lashed blue eyes widened.

Karen gasped. The lone diner was the ever-popular Emily Van Patten!

"Uh, hi, Karen," Emily said. Her translucent, perfect skin was stained red with embarrassment. It matched the small blob of ketchup on her lip.

"Hi," Karen said. She wanted to fall through the floor. What must Emily think, seeing her there all alone? "I'm meeting some friends," she added.

"Me, too," Emily said quickly.

Karen looked at what Emily was eating— cheeseburger deluxe, fries, onion rings, and a chocolate shake. This was not a meal for a girl who was waiting for friends to join her. No, this was definitely a meal for a girl trying to drown her sorrows in serious junk food.

Emily looked down at her plate, and her

blush deepened. "I'm hungry," she said in a small voice. She looked up at Karen. "When I was modeling I could never eat like this. I lived on yogurt and cottage cheese for weeks."

"I know just what you mean," Karen said, remembering the past week. "Dieting is rough."

"I thought you were with Ben tonight," Emily blurted suddenly.

"I was," Karen said shortly. There was no way she'd tell Emily that her dinner had been a fiasco. "We had a wonderful time," she said. Her voice sounded hollow, even to her.

A sudden flash of sympathy lit up Emily's deep blue eyes as she turned to Karen. "You look miserable," she said softly, and then instantly looked down. "I know the feeling."

Karen frowned as she studied the top of Emily's bent head. She'd never thought she could feel sorry for her rival, but Emily was obviously very sad. Almost as sad as Karen was. "Hey, Emily," she said gently. "Why don't you eat with me? I ordered a double helping of fries, and you've almost finished yours."

"I'll bring the mustard," Emily said, a slow smile spreading over her face as she stood.

Emily carried her food to Karen's table. There was an awkward pause. Then Karen smiled back at Emily, and both of them started in on the food. They devoured everything in record time, and then called the waitress back for another order of onion rings.

"This is the best I've felt in days," Emily said, swirling an onion ring in ketchup.

"Me, too," Karen agreed. "It's the best I've felt since——" She stopped guiltily.

Emily grinned. "Since I got back to town, right?"

"Right," Karen admitted, laughing. She put down a french fry and leaned over the table toward Emily. "Let's face it, Emily. Whose fault is it that we're so miserable?"

Emily wiped her mouth with her napkin. "Ben's," she said flatly. "Dating both of us at the same time was a ridiculous idea. It was guaranteed to drive us crazy."

"It was!" Karen exclaimed. "He's being completely insensitive."

"And there I was, giving you dirty looks at school, when it wasn't your fault at all," Emily said. "I'm sorry, Karen."

"I'm sorry, too," Karen admitted. "I was just as bad."

Emily bit her lip. "Look, I just want to say something. I didn't want to steal Ben away from you, Karen. But I had such a horrible time in New York I just *had* to come back to River Heights. I was written out of the series——I was pretty terrible."

"You were?" Karen asked incredulously.

Emily nodded. "Oh, yeah. Then my mother

was really pushing me to do more modeling, but I hated it. Plus, I really missed my dad. So somehow I got my mom to agree to let me live with him. She's happy in New York. Maybe she'll find her own career."

"But didn't you like New York?" Karen asked.

"I liked the city, I guess. I did have fun sometimes. But I hated the series. It was awful!" Emily exclaimed, shuddering. "I was nervous all the time. My stomach was in knots. Jason Monroe is a jerk. And I still hadn't gotten over my parents splitting up."

Karen nodded sympathetically. "It sounds awful." Suddenly, she had a whole new view of Emily Van Patten.

Emily straightened suddenly. "But let's get back to Ben. What are we going to do?"

"Well," Karen said thoughtfully, "Ben's decision to date both of us worked only because we agreed to it. What if we both put our feet down and say no? We're fed up. He can't see either of us until he makes up his mind."

Emily frowned. "Not see Ben?" she asked.

"It's the only way," Karen said determinedly. "We can do it, Em. Ben just has to choose. It's the only fair way."

"You're right," Emily agreed. "I thought things were bad in New York. I never thought I'd be a nervous wreck in River Heights!"

Karen stuck out her hand. "Is it a deal?"

Emily grinned and took her hand. Their

handshake was sticky with ketchup but firm with resolve.

"Deal," Emily said.

Karen got to the River Heights High parking lot right on time Saturday morning. She felt absolutely terrific. She hadn't gotten up early to set her hair, and she was pleasantly full from her breakfast of scrambled eggs and toast dripping with butter. She was dressed comfortably in a pretty sweater, skirt, and flats. She was the old Karen Jacobs, and she liked herself just fine.

She felt only a slight pang when she saw Emily arrive. Unfortunately, Emily hadn't gotten any less gorgeous overnight. She was wearing a luxurious camel coat and a thick pink muffler. With a big smile she weaved her way through the crowd of students toward Karen.

"Do we still have a deal?" Emily asked.

Karen nodded. "You bet. I just saw Ben pull in. We might as well get this over with."

Together they crossed the parking lot. Ben was obviously shocked to see Karen and Emily together. It was enough to make Karen smile, but she kept a straight face.

"Hi," he said nervously.

"Ben, Emily and I have a proposal for *you* now," Karen said crisply. "We want you to stop seeing us until you make up your mind."

Ben backed up a step and bumped into his car. "What?"

"You heard us," Emily said. "It isn't fair of you to pit us against each other. We feel as if it's a competition."

"But I never meant for you to feel that way," Ben protested. "I've been miserable."

"Good," Emily responded.

"We all have," Karen said flatly. "So it's got to stop. You can do your thinking on your own time. Emily and I won't date you, and we won't talk to you on the phone, either."

"That's right," Emily said firmly.

"When you decide," Karen continued, "just let us know."

"*If* we're still around," Emily added. "Ready, Karen?" She held out an arm.

Karen slipped her arm through Emily's. "Ready."

"But wait!" Ben sputtered. "Emily, you're supposed to sit next to me on the bus."

"Too bad," Emily said sweetly. "I'm sitting with Marshall Fitzgerald."

"And I'm sitting with Terry," Karen added.

"But—"

"So long, Ben," Karen and Emily said in unison.

Ben looked after them, his mouth flapping open in surprise.

Meanwhile, across the parking lot, Nikki pulled in with Robin and Lacey.

"Look at Ben Newhouse," Robin said, leaning forward and staring out the windshield. "He looks like he just ran into a brick wall. Do you know what's going on, Lacey? You had lunch with him the other day."

"Huh?" Lacey said. Her blue eyes were focused someplace in the distance. "Oh. I have no idea."

"How come Cal isn't coming today?" Nikki asked Robin as they got out of the car.

Robin giggled. "Cal thinks culture is something that grows in a petri dish." She laughed and turned toward Lacey, who was straight-faced. "Get it, Lacey? Culture, petri dish? Biology lab?"

"Oh," Lacey said. "Right."

Robin exchanged a worried glance with Nikki. Lacey had been quiet all morning. "What's wrong, Lacey?" she prodded.

Lacey's lower lip trembled. "I can't talk about it now, guys," she said in a wobbly voice. "I don't want to lose it in front of the whole school. But last night was the worst yet. I think, if things go on like this, Rick and I might even break up!"

13

Suzanne Ming finished her piano solo. The last note died away, and there was thunderous applause. Suzanne bowed to the audience with the composure of a seasoned performer. Then, as the applause continued, a grin flashed across her small face. It was gone almost as soon as it appeared, and she walked off the stage with the same perfect poise.

Nikki twisted in her seat to find Ellen. "Your sister was fabulous."

Tears were sparkling in Ellen's eyes. "I know," she whispered. "I'm so proud of her."

As polite applause began, Nikki faced forward again. Gillian St. James was walking across the stage. Her fair skin gleamed against a long black velvet gown. Her arms were graceful as she raised the violin to her shoulder. She was beautiful.

"Here we go," Niles muttered. Nikki studied him. His face was pale and his hands were clasped tightly in his lap.

The music began, the heartbreakingly lovely notes of the violin soaring through the concert hall. Nikki was no expert, but Gillian seemed to play flawlessly, with passion and precision. Her fingers flew over the strings, and her bow coaxed beautiful notes to spill into the air, tripping, sliding, and then reaching a soaring crescendo.

When Gillian finished playing, she bowed her head while the audience exploded in applause. Niles clapped so loud and so long that Nikki wondered if his hands hurt.

Everyone sat through the performances of several other young musicians from all over the world. Then there was a long wait while the jury conferred. Finally a man in a tuxedo stepped to the microphone and announced the winners. Suzanne Ming got honorable mention. Another violinist got third prize. A pianist took second prize. Then the man announced the winner: Gillian St. James.

Nikki clapped with the others. She was really happy for Gillian. Obviously, Gillian had worked hard and deserved the honor. And even if Niles had tears in his eyes as Gillian accepted the award, it didn't mean that he was in love with her.

Nikki trailed out of the auditorium behind the chattering crowd. Niles had rushed ahead to see if Gillian was already in the lobby, meeting her parents. By the time Nikki had pushed her way through the crush, the St. Jameses and the Butlers were all standing together in a corner of the lobby.

Nikki stopped. Niles had his arm around Gillian and was staring down at her with an expression on his face Nikki had never seen before. The reason she'd never seen it before, Nikki slowly realized, was that Niles had never looked at her in quite that way.

Suddenly Nikki's knees felt weak. She stumbled back a step. Niles didn't love her. She knew that now. He liked her, he cared about her, but it wasn't love.

Nikki stood stock-still in the middle of the crowd. She had to read her own heart carefully. She wasn't destroyed, she realized almost instantly. Why not? She remembered the pain when she'd decided Tim didn't love her anymore. Why didn't she feel that way about Niles?

Because I was never really in love with Niles at all, Nikki realized. The thought was so electrifying she felt as though she'd been struck by lightning.

Robin was right! Maybe it had been easy to convince herself she loved Niles because she'd always known he'd be leaving someday. She would never really have to follow through. Their romance always had limits. And no matter what Niles said, Gillian had always been in the background.

As if in a dream, Nikki watched as Niles headed across the lobby toward her. He was so handsome. She smiled as he approached, feeling free for the first time in a long while.

"Come on over," Niles said. "Gillian has been asking for you."

Nikki put a hand on his sleeve. "All right, but I want to talk to you first." She looked into his dark eyes. "Niles," she said carefully, "you still love Gillian, don't you?"

Niles was taken aback. He hesitated. "I guess I do," he said softly. "I didn't realize it until recently. I swear it, Nikki. I thought I was over her."

"I know," Nikki said. "It's okay, Niles, really. I understand. Does she know?"

Niles shook his head. "She thinks I'm in love with you," he said. "I thought I was."

"I thought I was in love with you, too," Nikki admitted. "And maybe we were, a little bit. But it's not the same as how you feel about Gillian, is it?"

"I care about you very much, Nikki," Niles

said, his dark eyes serious. "But, no, it's not quite the same."

Nikki smiled. "Friends?"

"Always." Niles leaned over and kissed her cheek. When he pulled away, he looked concerned. "Nikki, are you all right?"

Nikki tilted her head back and gave him a dazzling smile. "For some strange reason, Niles, I've never been better. Now let's go see Gillian so I can congratulate her—on *both* prizes. She's a very lucky girl."

Karen stood with Ellen, and Suzanne Ming and their parents. She hadn't had a chance yet to apologize to Ellen, but she didn't want to interrupt Suzanne's big moment. But when Suzanne took her parents over to talk to her music teacher from school, Karen was able to talk to Ellen alone.

"Ellen, I want to tell you something," she said. "I tried to call last night, but it got too late, and I knew Suzanne would be going to bed early. I'm really sorry about what happened at school the other day. Basically, I've been acting like a jerk. Things with Ben just drove me over the edge."

"It's okay, Karen," Ellen said with her soft smile. "I understand."

"It's *not* okay," Karen said. "I want you to know that I'm back to normal. Sort of," she added with a grin. "I mean, I'm still upset about Ben, but I'm not going to be his slave any longer. I don't think he liked it very much, anyway. Especially when I almost poisoned him last night."

Ellen tilted her head curiously, and Karen quickly told her the story of her disastrous dinner. Ellen laughed hardest when Karen got to the part about the walnuts.

"You poor thing," Ellen said, wiping a tear of laughter from her cheek. "But I'm really sorry about the dress. It shouldn't have ripped the first time you wore it. Maybe I can talk my mother into giving you your money back."

"That would be great," Karen said. "I don't deserve it, though."

Ellen glanced quickly at Emily. "I noticed Emily's been flirting with all the guys today," she said in a low tone. "She must be trying to make Ben jealous."

"I noticed, too," Karen agreed. Emily had been flirting outrageously, and Karen had caught Ben staring at her a lot. He might get jealous enough to choose Emily. Well, maybe it was a good plan, but flirting just wasn't Karen's style. All she could do was be herself. She'd learned that the hard way.

"I hope you win him back," Ellen told her.

"You know, it's funny," Karen said thoughtfully, "but I don't see it as a case of winning or losing anymore. I was thinking of this situation like some kind of war, but Ben can't help who he loves. Nobody can, right?"

"Right," Ellen agreed. Her eyes softened when she caught sight of Kevin Hoffman across the lobby. She giggled when he crossed his eyes at her.

Karen's grin slowly faded when she saw who was behind Kevin. Emily was no longer surrounded by admirers. She was talking to Ben. As Karen watched, Ben took her in his arms and hugged her.

He's made his choice, Karen thought numbly, her eyes locked on the two of them. He had chosen Emily!

"Ellen, I'll see you later," she mumbled. "I have to get a soda." She stumbled away in the opposite direction from Ben and Emily, heading for the exit. She needed fresh air desperately, and she had to be alone.

As soon as she was outside, Karen sank down on the marble steps of Orchestra Hall. The steps were freezing even through her coat. She placed her bare hands on the cold stone, hoping the shock would help to numb her.

She heard footsteps behind her, and she kept her face forward. She was going to cry, she knew it. Then the footsteps came closer, and she recognized Ben's loafers. He had come to say goodbye.

He sank down on the steps next to her. "Hi," he said.

Karen didn't answer. Her throat was too tight to get a word out, and she didn't want Ben to know she was close to tears.

"You and Emily really knocked me for a loop this morning," Ben said. "I guess I deserved it, but it made me realize something."

A tear rolled down Karen's cheek, but she didn't dare brush it away. Just tell me, Ben, she pleaded silently. Let's get it over with.

"Karen, you've been acting pretty crazy this past week," Ben went on. "I want you to know that I don't love you because you type my term papers or because you agree with me no matter what I say or even because you're such a terrible cook."

"Don't worry. I hung up my spatula for good." Karen forced the words out through her tight throat. Ben was making her feel worse than ever.

Then, suddenly, Karen realized what Ben had said. Her heart seemed to stop beating. He had said that he *loved* her. Or had he?

"What did you just say?" she asked.

Ben took her hand and laced his fingers through hers. "I told you that I love you," he answered. "And I love you because you're *you*—not some perfect girlfriend."

She turned to him. "But what about Emily?" she asked, wiping her cheek.

"I did love her," Ben admitted. "I guess I

always will, in a way. I thought I'd never get over her. And then," he said with a smile, "you came along. Things changed. Even when you told me you loved me, I couldn't trust my feelings."

Karen remembered with a shudder when she'd blurted out the truth to Ben. "Why not?" she asked.

Ben examined their entwined hands. "Because I don't like to think of myself as a fickle guy. I couldn't believe that I could fall in love with you so fast after Emily. But I did. And it was better than anything I ever had with her. She's a terrific girl, but something just feels so right with you, Karen. I can't explain it."

Tears filled Karen's eyes. "You don't have to," she whispered. "I know." She felt sorry for Emily. She must be hurting right now.

"You know, it's funny," Ben went on. "Seeing Emily with other guys just didn't bother me that much. Remember that day in the cafeteria when all those guys were at her table? I sat there wondering why I didn't feel bad. Then today I thought about how I'd feel if *you* were surrounded by guys. That would kill me." He squeezed her hand. "I'm sorry it took me so long to realize that."

"Only a week," Karen pointed out.

"Only a week? It felt like forever!" Ben exclaimed fervently. Then he asked worriedly,

"It's not too late, is it? Did I blow it with you for good?"

Karen smiled, but she really wanted to stand up and cheer. "Don't worry," she said, squeezing his hand. "I'm still here."

"I can't tell you how glad I am to hear that," Ben said. His brown eyes were tender as he reached over to brush a strand of hair away from her face. "I'm sorry I ever made you cry," he murmured.

"Everything's okay now," Karen said. She wished Ben would stop talking and just kiss her.

Ben smiled, as if he could read her thoughts. Well, maybe he could, Karen thought as her gaze tangled with his. He leaned over and kissed her, his warm mouth sending a familiar thrill through her. Everything was better than okay, Karen thought dreamily. Everything was perfect.

Nikki sat in the darkened theater, trying to concentrate on the action on stage. The Windy City Rep was putting on a great performance. The set was imaginative, and the two leads were excellent, but Nikki couldn't concentrate. All she could think about was that Tim's right arm was slightly touching her left shoulder. That knowledge kept her pulse racing and her brain whirling.

Nikki didn't know whether to laugh or cry.

It felt wonderful to know finally what she wanted. She'd been so wrong! For weeks now, she thought she'd been trying to get Tim Cooper out of her heart, but she never had been able to. He'd always been there, but she'd been too stubborn and blind to understand.

She sneaked a peek at him. He seemed to be concentrating on the stage. Lara, sitting on his left, noticed Nikki checking out Tim, and Nikki snapped her head forward again. Was Tim serious about Lara? Had Nikki lost him to her?

The scene that she and Tim would perform began. The passion of the couple rippled through the audience like a wave. As Nikki watched, she wondered again why Tim had picked that scene from that particular play. There were so many other plays he could have chosen. Had he been trying to give her a message?

Out of the corner of her eye, Nikki saw Lara slip her hand into Tim's. Tim held it for a moment, then shifted and crossed his arms. Nikki's heart lifted. Was that a good sign? She shook her head. You're pretty desperate, girl, she told herself ruefully.

On stage Rita and Lamont confessed their love. Things were so simple in the theater, Nikki thought. In a couple of hours everything could be resolved. Real life wasn't so easy.

Sometimes mistakes just couldn't be undone. Nikki sneaked another look at Tim. Should she confess to him that she wanted to try again? Or would that only lead to more heartbreak?

———————————

When Lacey and Rick's romance starts to crumble, she's drawn to his rebellious older brother. But what will Rick say when he finds out? Nikki still can't figure out how Tim feels about her. When he kisses her onstage in their big scene, is he just acting or is he for real? Find out in River Heights #12, *Hard to Handle.*

The Linda Stories

*Read all about the boys
in Linda's life...
from her first crush to
the ups and downs of
a powerful true love.*

☐ *We Hate Everything But Boys*   72225/$2.95
When Linda and her friends start the We Hate Everything But Boys club, watch out! They'll do *anything* to find out if the boys they like really like them, too. Have four boy-crazy girls ever caused so much trouble?

☐ *Is There Life After Boys*   69559/$2.95
It's a new year and Linda's at a new school...full of *girls*! In the meantime, back at P.S. 515, Sue-Ann is putting the moves on Linda's boyfriend! The situation seems hopeless until Linda meets Mark and discovers something wonderful...there's nothing like an older boy to mend a broken heart!

☐ *We Love Only Older Boys*   69558/$2.95
Linda loves Louie...that's what's tattooed all over Linda's heart. If only Louie would decide *he* loves *her*! Linda's best friends already have older boyfriends, but all *she's* got is boy trouble. Then Linda discovers the perfect solution to her problems—right under her nose!

continued

☐ *My Heart Belongs To That Boy*   70353/$2.95

When Linda and Lenny first get together, it's *wonderful*. This is real love, at last! But then Lenny starts cutting school and flirting with other girls, and the fireworks start! Linda still loves him, but she can't help but wonder...how will they ever get it right?

☐ *All For The Love Of That Boy*   68243/$2.95

After a summer apart, Linda is sure she and Lenny will never break up again. It's great to be back with her old crowd, and back in Lenny's arms again...until her friends start drifting apart, and Lenny pulls his craziest stunt ever. With everything changing so fast, will their love change, too?

☐ *Dedicated To That Boy I Love*   68244/$2.75

By senior year Linda knows it's true—Lenny is the love of her life. Even if he *does* still get into trouble sometimes, Linda is determined to stand by him. But then when Lenny finally finds a way to get his act together for good, Linda's world is turned completely upside down!

☐ *Loving Two Is Hard To Do*   70587/$2.95

Linda doesn't set out to have a summer romance...it just happens. Dave is handsome and smart, and he never gets into trouble like Lenny. Soon Linda is back in the city, though, and so is Lenny. She can't have them both...but how can she ever choose between them?